# 17 CLIPSTONE STREET

What happened to Sarah Gardom and her base born son
who disappeared from the little village of Edensor,
near Baslow in Derbyshire in 1785?

*Ann Carmichael*

## ANN CARMICHAEL

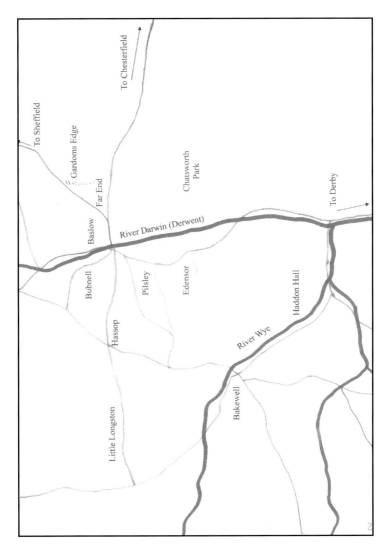

Published by Skimmia Publishing
ISBN 978-0-9927645-1-7

Printed by
Orphans Press
Leominster, Herefordshire, UK

*For Louise*

4

# CHAPTER ONE

**Edensor, near Baslow, Derbyshire in 1785**

"Can't you persuade Sarah to eat less; she's getting so fat. People will begin to talk."

John Gardom, or John of Bawkes as he was known, addressed his wife. Joyce burst into tears. She had been dreading this moment.

"Whatever is the matter, lass? What have I said?" He put his arms around his wife who was now sobbing uncontrollably. When she could eventually speak she said simply

"Sarah is with child."

John sat down. Although the thought had passed through his mind this was not what he wanted to hear; he had always been a reasonably even tempered man but he could feel his body heat rising and his pulse racing.

"Well, the young man must be brought to account and a marriage arranged as soon as possible." He was trying to keep calm.

"It's not as simple as that, John. Sarah won't say who the father is except that it's someone connected with the Big House and he's not in a position to marry her. What on earth are we going to do?"

In order to clear his head John needed to walk, find a rational solution. He was not aware that anyone else in his family, had been in this situation, but perhaps such things had escaped his notice. He had a big family and in order to provide well for them he worked hard at the blacksmithing just like his father and grandfather before him. They had a decent house and were well set up with a few acres to farm. He thought Sarah had looked so pretty at the wedding of cousin Elizabeth in March earlier that year. Why couldn't Sarah have found a nice young man like James Longsdon? Now what had she done? He dared not think who the father of her child might be; she had always been a handful, had a mind of her own, not placid like the other children. They should never have allowed her to go to the Public Days at nearby Chatsworth House but it was open to all: friends, tenants and any respectable stranger who happened to be passing by. It was such a sumptuous place stuffed full with beautiful furniture, fabulous paintings and ornamentation obviously meant to inspire awe amongst the ordinary people who trooped around and no doubt caused envy amongst the aristocracy. There had been such 'goings on' with Georgiana and her London friends but he had to admit that the Duchess had taken on her responsibilities looking after their tenants and local parishioners' needs without fault - those who needed charity received food or alms.

John walked round his flock of sheep counting them automatically without really seeing them. Perhaps they could come to some sort of arrangement with the father, whoever he was. He was not looking forward to speaking to his daughter about the matter but it would have to be dealt with as patiently as possible. What a bumblebroth. It was no good losing his temper but he did feel angry, terribly let down and, above all else, concerned for his dear wife, Joyce.

He had been walking, head down, deep in thought until he suddenly found himself by the awesome clump of ancient beech trees on Calton Pastures, a rich plateau of land where his grandfather had kept sheep. He wondered how long the magnificent trees had been there, who planted them, what stories could they tell. He carefully picked his way back along the path, taking more notice of his surroundings and stopped abruptly when he almost tripped over a hare that had been playing and frisking with her leveret. When she finally perceived John she stood up and pricked her ears staring straight at him and the little leveret darted into some thick scrub whilst the hare slunk stealthily away being very wary until out of sight. He reached the stile and climbed over; to his right he could see the magnificent Chatsworth House with the hunting tower behind. His grandfather and namesake, the well-known Ironmaster, had crafted beautiful ironwork and his great uncle, Sam Watson, had worked continuously for twenty years carving stone and wood for the Devonshires. 'Damn the place' he thought irrationally. He skirted Edensor village and was home with a clearer head before nightfall. He later cuddled Joyce in bed and told her that everything would be alright.

It was decided that Sarah should give birth to her baby at home. Her son, John, was christened in Edensor Church in October, 1785. Shortly afterwards Mother and baby left the village for good.

# CHAPTER TWO

## James and Elizabeth Longsdon, Little Longstone Manor - 1813

"You should see the farmhouse that Sarah Gardom's misbegotten son is living in.....plenty of ground around it and in the best street in Bolsover.... so young and obviously doing well for himself. I saw him in the market selling cows and followed him home.......kept my distance, he didn't see me. That's why I'm late." Elizabeth looked up from her cooking as her husband James Longsdon burst in through the kitchen door, obviously longing to tell her his news.

"How do you know it was him?" she said as she gave him a kiss. "Tell me first and then for heaven's sake go and take a bath; it's all ready for you and Madge can easily heat some more water on the scullery range. You are dirty and smelly!"

"The auctioneer called out his name - John Gardom - and a nice bunch of cattle they were too. I noticed he was a bit slow handing over the luck money but he didn't go straight in the ale house like a lot of them do ...... straight back home to his wife. She opened the door to him, babe in arms and another at her feet. What happened to his mother? You and she used to be good friends. I remember her at our wedding; not a bad looking lass."

"Oh James I wish I knew. I have thought of her frequently and it's so sad that she left Edensor with her little son without saying goodbye and then her mother, Joyce, died about three years later. The whole thing must have broken her heart."

"Is supper ready, only I thought I'd pop up to the Packhorse for a quick drink" queried James.

"I do know there's a new barmaid" Elizabeth chuckled "and yes, supper is ready. Besides, I'd have thought you'd have been too tired after your long ride back from Bolsover."

Well that's scotched that, thought James, for the time being, anyway.

Later on during supper they continued their conversation.

James was saying: "Bolsover's a funny place. Granted it's a thriving market town and most of the new houses are very attractive but its history goes way back to William dePeverell who gained the manor because he was a prominent supporter of William the Conqueror and claimed he was his illegitimate son. Later the manor was granted to George Talbot who became the sixth Earl of Shrewsbury. Eventually it came into the hands of Charles Cavendish of Welbeck whose descendants, the Dukes of Portland, remain the Lords of the manor of Bolsover to the present day."

"I've heard there is a castle" said Elizabeth.

"Yes, that's right. Originally it was a Norman fortress built on top of a hill but Cavendish pulled it down and built a mansion. Imagine what it was like when Charles I was entertained there - the music, the pageantry, and the banquets."

"Well" said Elizabeth "it can't have been the time to build a fortress as had been the need five hundred years before."

"It's generally thought that the main intention of Sir Charles was to recreate the atmosphere of times gone by. That he succeeded is there for all to see and although the castle has battlements and turrets it also has two pretty cupolas, picturesque riding stables and rooms with names like the Star Chamber and the Heaven Room."

James had had a long day, but with interesting tales to tell his wife. Now her mind was full of questions about Sarah and her son and she needed to think carefully about what action she could take to contact them but she didn't know where to start. She knew that both Sarah's parents had died and were buried in Edensor churchyard. Heaven knows what had happened to her siblings – they'd probably all gone their separate ways when the 6th Duke of Devonshire had decided to move the village as it spoilt his view from Chatsworth House. She'd been so busy raising her own family, the years had flown by and she'd lost touch with her Gardom cousins even though they lived only a few miles away.

Meanwhile she had to remember where she had safely stored the sunflower seeds and other grains to be used for her collage which she had offered to make for the well dressing ceremony at the end of July. It was good to commemorate the fact that they had a supply of clean fresh water. She would have to start sketching one or two possible designs for it and most probably incorporate some flower petals which she had started to save and dry carefully. Somewhere she had some small alder cones too which were a good standby in case she couldn't dry enough rose petals which perished so quickly, but she didn't need to worry as there was always a spectacular show of a variety of blooms in her garden. Although Derbyshire was a cold place to live she was very proud of her walled flower garden which lay to the front and side of the house. It was sheltered from the cold winds and had been a safe place for the children to play.

***

The Longsdon family were established in Little Longstone from the 13th century but their fortunes improved in the early 17th century when they exchanged lands with the Countess of Shrewsbury, 'Bess of Hardwick'. By this they gained access to common and woods and free grazing on Longsdon Moor for 200 sheep. The family benefited by the wool trade so that when Elizabeth Gardom married into the family they had 450 acres of rented land and 150 freehold acres.

Little Longstone Manor is one of the most beautiful stone built houses one could wish to see. The wide two storey gabled Elizabethan house with pretty chimneys and stone mullioned windows sits quietly in walled gardens within its landscape protected by rising ground to the rear and with lovely views over pastureland to the front. It was here that James and Elizabeth raised their family. Elizabeth was the daughter of Johnathan Gardom of Bubnell Hall, a successful business man and owner of Calver cotton mill and she had married James Longsdon in March 1785. By way of dowry Johnathan had covenanted £1500.00 (at least £160,000 today) on the marriage and the same amount on the first birthday of the first surviving child. He may have been prompted to do this as his first wife had given birth to three sons who each only survived a short time and she had died shortly after the birth of the last surviving child of the marriage.

Elizabeth Longsdon bore her husband three sons – James, John and William – and two daughters who were Elizabeth and Katherine. The three boys boarded for their schooling and their parents wrote regular affectionate letters to them always expressing pleasure in the knowledge that the boys were in good health and making satisfactory progress with their books. James senior always included snippets of information about how the farm crops were doing and what livestock he had traded.

Through the years it is apparent that they were a close knit and loving family who corresponded with one another when separated. Elizabeth was frequently sending warm clothing and food parcels to her sons. James senior was often expressing his wish that his eldest son was with him to help with the livestock and the running of the farm.

The activities of James Longsdon included buying cattle for fattening from fairs in Derbyshire and Lancaster and like Elizabeth's father he also became involved in the cotton industry being in partnership with the Morewood family of Alfreton, High Peak. Together they opened a trading agency in St. Petersburg, once capital of the Russian Empire and one of the chief ports. There was little manufacturing there but the port had become the export harbour for more than half Russia and foreigners rushed there to take advantage of the growing export trade. But it was a place of no traditions, no interesting history beyond that of the palace conspiracies and nothing in its past really to attract investigation. Furthermore, concentration of political power was in the hands of an absolute Government and in the narrow circles surrounding the chief of state. Who would have wanted to linger in such a cold, wet, inhospitable place?

In England when Richard Arkwright's patent claims were dismissed the Longsdon and Morewood Partnership decided to expand their interests in cotton manufacturing. They built a carding mill (where cotton fibres were combed off) and warehouse, plus a bleaching croft in Great Longstone, but after two years the partnership was dissolved.

It appears that James Longsdon senior had engaged in some ill-advised business ventures and it was revealed in one letter that James junior wished his father would stick to farming activities!

However, when his eldest son, John, was twenty one years old he was with Messrs. Forsyth, Smith & Company establishing an agency in Nova Scotia. What was the attraction of making a sea voyage of at least 45 days to Nova Scotia, (New Scotland) an island off the coast of Canada surrounded by the Atlantic Ocean? The young man was so brave to risk illness and indeed his life aboard one of the sturdy little packet ships; the level decked types with a galley were best with a long boat securely lashed between the fore and main masts and in which carried livestock pens for sheep, ducks, geese and chickens. The cow house was lashed over the main hatch with other small hatch houses and a wooden shelter (companion) leading to the comfortable well-appointed cabins with skylights and lit by candles and whale oil lamps. Steerage passengers lived in the between-decks placed amidship and the crew's living quarters were in the forepeak of the ship. Stores, spare sails and gear were kept in the lazaretto behind the stern cabins which had a small hatch leading to the main deck. These little sailing ships were the only regular means of communication across the Atlantic and were tossed about on the sea speeding with all their might making journeys through the ice and fogs of summer and in the winter through snow, sleet and gales. Their captains were the most competent men available and were responsible for the lives of eminent men and women, government documents, mail and coinage.

As they sailed into the port of Halifax John Longsdon saw hanging and rotten corpses of pirates and in particular Edward Jordan. He had been a passenger on the 'Three Sisters' who took control of the schooner and viciously murdered several men. When Jordan was eventually captured he was hanged and left on the gallows as a warning to others contemplating piracy.

A country rich in mineral deposits such as granite, slates, limestone, bituminous coal of rich quality, many types of ore, copper, silver and gold in workable quantities were the foundations of new industry. Not only being surrounded by the sea but the interior of the country was traversed and watered by many rivers and lakes and gave rise to a rich source of fish; Nova Scotia was one of the largest and most valuable fisheries in British North America. Although there were extremes of heat and cold the climate, being coupled with good soil, created the right conditions for a valuable agricultural land where cereals, pulses, root crops and fruit were cultivated - even grapes and peaches grew outside in some districts. The forests were extensive and valuable and successful timber trade was created. There was a variety of livestock, the contours of the land affording good shelter during inclement weather. John Longsdon didn't find it a strong manufacturing country but the diversity was immense and every year new industries were added such as sugar refining and cotton manufacturing. What was eventually made in considerable quantities were coarse 'home-spuns,' coarse flannels, bed linen, blankets, carpets and tweeds - products that could offer trading opportunities for experienced business people like the Longsdons who were already engaged in the cotton industry in England and were prepared to take all the risks involved.

John Longsdon travelled from Nova Scotia across the Northumberland Strait to Prince Edward Island and recorded his journey in a letter to his brother James:

'Complaining that he had not heard from him but assumed all his time was taken up with the local civilian army and cattle trading. John left Halifax on 28th June 1809 and eventually arrived at Puton 110 miles away. He was delayed one day by rain and the roads were very bad. He stayed with an acquaintance from Ashbourne and then he sailed about twenty eight leagues in a small boat for Prince Edward Island, was becalmed, then in a storm. He walked two hours before breakfast then a further ten miles then rested because it was ninety degrees in the shade, lying on the floor, all beds being occupied. He reached Charlotte-town next evening. He spent twelve hours very unpleasantly, getting business done as best he could. He returned to Halifax arriving on Wednesday July 19th. Prince Edward Island had been wooded but the timber was no longer of any value because the settlers had cleared and burnt. He gave an account of meals of which breakfast was the best. There was a great plenty of fish which was the principal dish. He was travelling to Boston (USA) the next day and expected to arrive in eight days' time. He had just heard news from New York that the French had been defeated. He ended his letter by saying that if he returned in October he might visit New York.'

The Longsdon business eventually devolved on the three brothers and for several years they had dealings with their Gardom relatives; uncles Thomas and George Gardom of Bubnell were supplying them with cotton hosiery. Trading difficulties led to James junior withdrawing from the cotton manufacturing industry but his two brothers later went on to develop a textile merchants business in Charleston, South Carolina.

If nothing else this generation of the Longsdon family certainly had an adventurous spirit always willing to try something new. Perhaps some of the entrepreneurial spirit of their grandfather Johnathan Gardom had influenced them. He was a hosier and yarn merchant, nephew of John the Ironmaster (who had crafted beautiful ironwork at Chatsworth, Castle Howard and other prominent properties). His parents were Thomas and Elizabeth (nee Broomhead) whose family home was the beautiful Bubnell Hall near Baslow. Not only did he have a daughter, Elizabeth, but three sons William, George and Thomas. A widower, Jonathan had married in 1771 an agreeable widow lady from Youlgrave, by the name of Christian Chappell. This lady had a fortune inherited from her former husband, John Denman, physic of Bakewell.

By way of the marriage the family had money to invest in a new venture. News of Arkwright's intention to build a mill in the area may have prompted Jonathan into partnership with John Pares of Leicester who was a banker and who was also involved in the hosiery trade. The two men decided that instead of buying spun yarn for their stocking makers to knit, they could spin it themselves. With all their business connections they thought that they would have a ready market for their yarn. In about 1778 they came to an agreement with Jeddediah Strutt and Richard Arkwright to licence the use of water-powered spinning frames and carding engine, a machine that disentangled, cleaned and intermixed fibres to produce a continuous web suitable for processing. The cost for the use of the machines was a colossal amount and added to this the licensees had to agree not to divulge the patents and not to use the machines beyond a stipulated number of hours. At the same time Gardom and Pares took a twenty one year lease from Thomas Eyre of Hassop on land at Calver Bridge. In place of a corn mill they rapidly constructed a three story cotton mill. Before the patents on the machines were due to expire Crompton's Mule (a machine for spinning cotton) emerged as an alternative to Arkwright's water frame and it had the very significant advantage of being unencumbered by patents. In the summer of 1781 Arkwright's carding patent was successfully challenged but the legal tussles with the two business men went on and on and the patent was reinstated in 1785 only for the decision to be reversed a few months later. Pares began constructing a much larger mill at Calver and there was another mill at Caton. They were in dispute with Arkwright over royalty payments added to which Jonathan Gardom had ignored some of the terms of the licence and was unwilling to pay the fees for the money he had loaned from Arkwright whilst the status of the patents remained uncertain. Despite the exorbitant start-up costs Gardom and Pares were successful.

Calver, a village mentioned in the Domesday Book of 1086, is situated on low ground of the Derwent Valley and the earliest settlement probably began near the river Derwent where several ancient east to west trading routes forded the river. Since the middle ages this ancient way was used by jaggers (people transporting loads) leading the pack-horse teams across the river, sometimes with up to forty heavily laden animals, before climbing the steep eastern bank up through Curbar Gap and on across the Big Moor to Leash Fen to the towns of Sheffield and Chesterfield. The settlement became more important following the building of the first Calver Bridge in pre-Tudor times, which replaced the earlier hazardous ford, coupled with the commencement of lead mining in the sixteen hundreds. Calver prospered from the development of local quarrying, lead-smelting and lime burning and with the new industry eventually a new road – the Chesterfield to Wardlow Mires Turnpike – was built in 1759.

Sadly, Jonathan Gardom died in 1788 leaving his sons and John Pares to take over the business in Calver.

For some years the business was successful but tragedy struck when in 1799 the three hundred years old Calver Bridge was swept away during the disastrous floods. However, they set to work to clear up and repair the damage but the mill was hardly back in production when tragedy struck again. William Gardom, aged 49, cotton spinner of the 'Bleaching Yard House'

Bubnell Hall

died leaving a widow, Mary, and two young children to be provided for. William's will had hurriedly been written a few days before he died leaving his share in the Calver Mill business to his friend Horatio Mason and his brother-in-law Nicholas Broomhead of Cockhill.

Then in 1802 the larger of the two cotton mills burnt down completely. Many men might have given up at that point but the Gardom family and John Pares obviously decided that they would not be beaten; they built a new mill that would withstand any force of nature. The new six-storey building which dominated the little village had gritstone walls up to three feet thick. Not only did they rebuild the bridge and Calver Weir to hold back the water but a shuttle house which housed the sluice machinery to control the water, and a goit which channelled water to turn the mill wheels which powered the factory machinery. This gave the mill all the water power it needed and cotton continued to be spun at Calver for another ninety years but no-one became rich there.

George Gardom died in 1813 and his brother Thomas in 1817. Their surviving children decided to cut their losses and relinquish their interest in the business. When John Pares retired in 1824 the mill passed into the hands of Horatio Mason who lived with his family in the mill house. He was a benevolent and hard-working man concerned for the welfare of the employees, many coming from neighbouring villages, others living near the mill and he was intent on making beneficial changes for his workers.

Before the factories in England were built most cotton workers had worked at home but in the noisy, muggy factory atmosphere they worked 12 to 14 hour shifts often having to clean the machinery during meal-times. If there was the tiniest speck of dirt left on the machines the workers were fined. Their wages were a pittance and many owners preferred to employ women and children as they were cheaper than men. As soon as boys reached adulthood many were sacked and had to be supported by their families. The discipline was cruel to the extreme; punishment by leather strapping was not unheard of, children would have iron weights hung round their necks or they might be hung from the roof in baskets, or even have their ears nailed to the table. And of course, they were frequently dowsed in water buts to keep them awake. Fines were not only imposed for dirty machinery but for talking, whistling and leaving the room without permission even to obey a call of nature where the privies were a shared facility. Some employers demanded that their overseers raised a certain amount in fines each week. In some factories – not necessarily at Calver – children were forced to crawl into dangerous unguarded machinery to free trapped thread which led to horrendous accidents; many suffered head injuries and lost fingers. The loud noise made by the machines damaged workers' hearing. The air was full of dust which led to lung and chest diseases. Cotton thread had to be spun in damp, warm conditions; leaving the factory the pale sallow skinned workers, stooped and bent with deformed spines and thin limbs went straight out into the cold which led to many cases of pneumonia. In some city cotton mills orphans were apprenticed to owners, supposedly to learn the textile trade. Those poor, deprived children worked 12 hour shifts and slept in barracks attached to the factory in beds just vacated by other children about to start the next shift.

But Horatio Mason at Calver was one of the early reformers. Educational facilities were provided for the children, a Sunday school was established and working conditions were generally less harsh than in many other factories of the time. Some years later the cotton mill employed 200 workers.

Jonathan Gardom had prospered. His business interests had included returns on patents, mining ventures, farm produce, potash (potassium carbonate) manufacture together with the production of cotton, silk and worsted materials. He had been involved with the Ashford Marble Works, in existence for many years from 1748. At some stage, probably after marrying Christian Chappell, they moved from Bubnell Hall (where his son, Thomas, continued to reside) to live further up the lane at Bubnell House (or Bubnell Old Hall as it was known) a house richly steeped in history dating back to Medieval times.

# CHAPTER THREE

## Christopher Gardom

"Of course, the other person in my family who disappeared was Christopher" Elizabeth told her husband, James, as they sat well wrapped up almost inside the big stone fireplace in Little Longstone Manor one evening. They had been eating hot buttered oatcakes, licking their fingers and trying not to drop bits all over the hearth.

"What was that all about?"

She told him as much as she could remember of the episode as had been passed on to her through her family.

Anna Gardom, at the age of thirty six, had been left a widow with eight children in 1713. She had been married to John the Ironmaster, brother of Elizabeth's grandfather, Thomas. But when she married not only did Anna take on a husband but also her widower father-in-law, and John's brothers - Thomas who was eighteen and six years old Christopher. (Their mother had died giving birth to Christopher). Anna looked after them all and it must have been such hard work at times, and so harrowing especially when her father-in-law went blind and then during the last two years of her husband's life when his illness was so debilitating. It transpired that when he died John had made no provision in his will for his young brother Christopher who had been a tower of strength to Anna but by then was twenty six years of age and hadn't left the family home to find his own way in the world. However, Anna remarried a couple of years later and by all accounts her new husband, Richard Oddy, was a dashing gentleman a few years her junior. What is more, he took on all her seven surviving children and they moved into their new home in Bubnell. (Richard was another Ironmaster who had been commissioned by John Sheffield - 1st Duke of Buckingham - to craft railings and gates at Buckingham House in London). Anna must have been ecstatic, but the next day after the wedding the old family home which they had just left, Woodhouse at Far End, underneath Gardom Edge, burnt to the ground and Christopher disappeared. Apparently, the new bride was determined that these events would not overshadow their lives.

When Anna moved from Woodhouse to Bubnell Old Hall with Richard the elderly family retainer, Dorothy Howard, decided to stay in her cottage at Far End. She had worked for the family all her life but was too old to move. A few days after the fire she realised that some of her fowls had vanished at intervals, one by one. She knew it wasn't a fox which would have maimed and killed the lot, taken what it wanted and left the rest. She mentioned it to her neighbour, Ezra Cook and he said he thought it was strange but it seemed someone had been helping themselves to his garden produce. They didn't tell anyone, not for a long time. Old Ezra had worked for the Gardom family too and every day he walked round the fields looking at the Gritstone sheep. He could still spot something in trouble but he was too arthritic to catch anything with his crook like he used to. One day he was aware of tracks made by a horse. He followed the trail of hoof marks to an old field barn where there were sure signs of someone living rough. He and Dorothy thought it must be Christopher so the kind old lady began baking the odd pie or two, which Ezra took to the barn. Dorothy had been known to say it was terrible how his family treated him; he was such a dear little boy. This went on for a few weeks and then eventually the pies were left, uneaten. Whoever it was had gone.

But that wasn't the end of the story.

A few years later in 1726, Richard Oddy had quite a few problems to deal with. He was very, very happy with Anna. He had known many beautiful women in London but their beauty was artificial, they had too much wealth and their lives seemed to have little meaning. When he had first met Anna he had been captivated by her natural beauty, her fresh complexion and her contentment with her role in life. His ready-made family had all now married and his own son, Richard, was ten years of age. When John Gardom had died, because his eight children were too young to inherit, guardians had sensibly been appointed for them, the most prominent of these being his brother Thomas Gardom married to Kate Broomhead; they lived at Bubnell Hall with Kate's aunt who lived to the age of ninety. It was so unexpected and a terrible blow when Thomas died leaving a wife with five young children, the youngest, Johnathon (who became Elizabeth Longsdon's father), the only son being just a year old. Naturally, Richard and Anna were only too happy to give help and support especially as they lived such a short distance away along the lane. Richard, upon marrying Anna had happily taken on the responsibility of her children (he loved children) and then, unexpectedly, was a father figure to the children of Thomas as well.

The oldest son of John Gardom and Anna was Chris (they called him Kit), a very bright young man, who, at the age of twenty-one had inherited the farm under Gardom Edge and his step-father Richard was always happy to help out if he could. Of course there was no longer a farmhouse but the old stone farm buildings remained and temporary living accommodation was easily created if required; Richard had warned Anna that he might have to stay through the night - it was lambing time and he had ridden up from home in Bubnell early that morning through the shroud of mist savouring that quiet time before the rest of the world awakens. There had already been some multiple births but one or two ewes had died and he really didn't know how to deal with it, especially not then. He had a crisis on his hands; the family were all in shock. Two days before Kit had fallen from his horse when it reared up suddenly as a pheasant noisily took flight from the undergrowth. There was nothing that could be done, the young man's neck was broken and he died instantly. The farm-hand who was with him was still in a terribly agitated state. Kit's wife was due to give birth to their first child in a matter of days. It was a devastating situation but Richard had to deal with the matter in hand. He removed the bridle, unsaddled his horse and turned the sturdy animal out to a nearby paddock to graze as he anticipated that his return home would not be for some time. He walked quietly across to where the ewes had all been brought into the stone walled yard so at least he didn't have to go wandering round the fields looking for them as had been the custom. Then he noticed that three ewes with their lambs had been separately penned up with wooden hurdles; he had no recollection of doing that. And then he could not believe his eyes. A man with his back to him was down on his knees very quietly and skilfully assisting a ewe who was licking dry her firstborn whilst the second one was then carefully and swiftly extracted with the umbilical cord wrapped round its neck. The man quickly cut the cord, tickled the lamb's nose with a bit of straw which got it breathing with a shudder and placed the little creature close to its mother to nurture. Richard had watched spellbound. The man then seemed to dip his hands into a nearby bucket of grease and without any apparent distress to the ewe he extracted another lamb which even Richard could see was dead. It was then obvious that the man knew that Richard was there as he turned to him and said "I'll just pen them up. She's very tired after all that struggling.

The first one was twisted and the second was backwards. It's a wonder she and all her lambs aren't dead."

As the astonished Richard drew near to help with the hurdles the man's floppy felt hat fell off revealing a head of blond curly hair and then recognition dawned. It was John Gardom's youngest brother Christopher. Neither man knew what to say for a minute then both spoke at once.

"You've come back."

"I had to come back. I heard about Kit. I had to come."

There hadn't been time to think of anything. "Will you help me, Christopher, there is so much to do and I'm really quite inexperienced with the practicalities of lambing?" Richard had asked.

But Christopher was already assisting the next ewe and had replied "You make up the pens and I'll look after the sheep. We'll need some water from the brook and more straw. Oh, and yes, some nice hay for the ewes, the best you've got."

Richard had never laboured so hard in all his life. As Christopher worked quietly and competently he explained that after a difficult lambing some ewes rejected their lambs and by penning them up there was better chance of bonding and no risk of miss-mothering by other ewes. Neither would foxes be so keen to steal a weak lamb. One ewe then dropped a dead lamb and using a sharp knife he quickly skinned it, took a triplet from another ewe which he 'dressed' in the dead lamb's skin and put it to suckle on the bereft ewe. There was a bit of complaining for a while but both ewes soon settled down. Good strong ewes and lambs were turned back out into the field; there was no point keeping them in the yard.

There were obviously questions running through the minds of both men but no opportunity to voice them until nightfall when it looked as if no more births were imminent. They were both ravenous. Within the shelter of one of the old stone buildings the two men made themselves comfortable in the straw and shared the bread, cheese and ale that Anna had provided. Richard let the younger man reveal his story.

Christopher said that it wasn't his fault. He didn't start the fire but he thought that everyone would blame him. He didn't know what to do - stayed around for a while living rough - but then he thought that Anna had looked so happy in Church on her wedding day. He was so jealous of Richard having all of them, Anna and her children. He was afraid of his own feelings and decided to go as far away as possible. For a couple of years he just wandered with his mare and worked on farms where he could get something casual before moving on to the next place. Once, when he was sleeping rough he was set upon by drunken louts; they tried to rob him but he had few possessions. As long as his mare was safe that was all he cared about; his cuts and bruises soon healed. Another time he worked for a widow who thought she could pay him 'in kind' but there was no way he was going to 'bed' such an ugly old hag and he moved on from there very quickly! People were mostly very kind and appreciated his work. All he wanted was food, a bed and a reasonable wage.

Eventually he settled only a few miles away in Dronfield because he met such a lovely lass. He used to go down to a quiet spot of the river to swim. One evening he watched a mother otter and her three cubs playing in the water; it was such a lovely sight. Then he glimpsed something even more beautiful - a bathing pale skinned nymph-like creature with long flowing tresses totally unaware of her observer. He returned to that spot for several evenings hoping to catch sight of her again. When she spoke he almost fell off the river bank into the water.

"You like watching the otters play, too" she had said simply from somewhere behind him. "I'm Rachel; must get back home before I'm missed."

She totally befuddled him and needless to say that when he saw her again she easily coaxed him into the water. How could he resist? They played and frolicked like the otters which, unsurprisingly, had long since gone. Rachel gave him a reason to improve his life. He got a job as a shepherd; it was a big flock and there was plenty of demand for the wool right there. It was a thriving place with spinning, weaving, dying and tanning. Rachel and Christopher got married and moved in with her parents who were soap makers on the river banks. It's a closely guarded secret making soap. Christopher discovered that the lanolin extracted from wool used by soap makers, if applied to his hands, helped with difficult lambing.

They never had any children.

One day, he drank a little too much ale and told Rachel about his life at Woodhouse. He was only six when Anna married his big brother John. He didn't remember his mother because she died giving him birth, but of course his father was still at home organising the quarry and the building works and along with John and his other brother Thomas worked all the daylight hours. John was a very talented blacksmith and often went away for weeks at a time working at grand houses and big estates where they wanted fancy iron work. Anna brought Christopher up; she was special and educated him and his life was very happy. Then John and Anna had children but he was still part of the family. Because he didn't want to leave Woodhouse, to leave the life he had always known, Anna helped him to improve the farm and make a contribution to the family business. He imagined that he was settled there for life. In all reality he hadn't given the state of affairs enough thought; he had just muddled on in his own naïve way. It was a terrible shock when his brother John died to discover that there was no provision for him. There was no place for him. Kit, because he was the oldest son of John and Anna was to inherit everything. The guardians said that he could stay on and work for the family as a labourer but that he would not have any right to ownership of anything. That was too much for him to comprehend and he knew that he could not stay and be happy.

Eventually Christopher told Rachel about the fire because she guessed something more had happened to separate him from his family for so long. She thought he should return but he was undecided. Well, he had said that people gossip and talk about events and the news quickly reached him about Kit. That settled it. He went back and told Richard Oddy that he belonged there and somehow he knew there would be a job for him.

Christopher Gardom was welcomed back into his family. Rachel soon joined him and they lived out the rest of their days in what had been Dorothy Howard's cottage.

# CHAPTER FOUR

## John Binns - January, 1830

William opened the letter. It was addressed to his mother, Elizabeth Longsdon at Little Longstone Manor, but sadly she, his father and two brothers had all died. A London resident, John Binns of 52 Windsor Terrace, City Road had written in January, 1830 to say that their relative, Sarah Gardom, had died at the end of 1829 and wished them to know that she had been well treated and had, for the most part, enjoyed an interesting life in the metropolis. As William sometimes spent time in London on business matters he decided to meet the said John Binns. He felt regret that his mother had never made the effort to find and visit Sarah as they had been friends as young women. If he had known of Sarah's whereabouts perhaps he could have done something worthwhile in getting the two cousins to make contact. But now it was too late.

First of all he needed to establish who this person was as the name was very familiar to him but he couldn't immediately think why. However, his enquiries quickly revealed that a John Binns was connected with the London Corresponding Society. Surely Sarah hadn't been involved with that? It is thought that the French Revolution, which started as a desire for a more democratic society but then, by chance, put an end to the French monarchy, inspired people to want equal rights for all. The LCS were a group of people concentrating on the reform of Parliament and the original instigators were John Frost, an attorney, and Thomas Hardy, a shoemaker with radical beliefs. Membership predominantly consisted of artisans and working men and with groups, not only in London but in Manchester,

Norwich, Sheffield and Stockport. The society opposed England's wars with France and some of the members became involved with a reform group in Edinburgh organised by 'Friends of the People.' In 1793 a convention was broken up and a number of men were arrested and tried for sedition with the result that two representatives of the London Corresponding Society, Gerrald and Maragot, were sentenced to fourteen years transportation. The remaining LCS leaders were undaunted and met with other reformist groups to discuss a further national convention as well as to produce large numbers of pamphlets and periodicals. The Government decided to take more action and certain of the Society members were arrested and committed to the Tower of London charged with high treason which carried a maximum sentence of death by being hanged, drawn and quartered. Although, initially, the pressure from the Government for a guilty verdict was intense it was a very sensitive situation. They could not risk a trial by jury which produced a guilty verdict resulting in such a barbaric punishment as this would have fuelled even more cause for revolt. The Prime Minister, William Pitt, took the unusual step of questioning the accused LCS members who were defended by the lawyer Thomas Erskine. Three of the charged men, Thomas Hardy, John Thelwell and John Horne Tooke were tried, but the prosecution case was unsound and they were acquitted. The LCS members continued with their desires for legal equality with more public meetings; one near Copenhagen House in Islington was attended by a few thousand people. The mood of the people was so angry that the carriage of King George III was stoned as he went to open parliament.

"Oh dear, oh dear, oh dear" William muttered to himself.

"Whatever is the matter, William" queried Lizzie as she entered the study.

"I'm reading about John Binns. This is dreadful – however did Sarah get mixed up in all this?"

"I thought you'd like a little glass of brandy, a night-cap, but I'll leave you in peace…..don't stay up too late….. night, night" and she gave him a sisterly kiss on his cheek. William continued with his reading.

The government reacted with the "Two Acts" which was an extension of the treason laws, the Treasonable Practices Act and the restraining Seditious Meetings Act of 1795. Detention without trial had already been in force for a year; no writ was required to bring a prisoner before a court even to ascertain the legality of his or her confinement. In 1796 leading LCS members John Binns and John Gale Jones were arrested. Eventually Binns was successfully defended by Samuel Romilly against a charge of seditious words, but Gale Jones was found guilty at Warwick although never sentenced.

The Seditious Meetings Act made the organisation of parliamentary reform gatherings extremely difficult. Debating clubs writing letters to one another and periodically organizing demonstrations of a few thousand people seemed an unlikely cause for fear amongst the ruling classes but with the alarming circumstances of the French revolution the Government saw no option but to persuade Parliament to pass a Corresponding Societies Act which finally happened in 1799. It then became illegal for the LCS to meet and the organisation came to an end.

William Longsdon was feeling very apprehensive about his forthcoming meeting with John Binns and almost wished he had not opened the letter to his mother.

\*\*\*

A little hand gently touched his arm "Papa, I cannot sleep." William had nodded off in his comfortable winged armchair in front of the fire. It was his little daughter, Emma Jane.

"Come and sit on my lap and tell me your troubles."

"Charles has told me that he has seen gypsies in the wood and that they kidnap little children. Papa, I'm frightened. He's seen them sitting round their big black cauldron on their camp fire."

"Has he indeed; he shouldn't frighten you like that. I'm sure they are very kind people and they've probably poached a few rabbits for their cook-pot – no harm in that. Shall we all visit them tomorrow? Now, would you like me to tell you a story and then you can go back to bed" and the child was soon asleep in his arms.

\*\*\*

As soon as he was able William made further enquiries about John Binns and learnt that he was known to be a journalist with radical beliefs who was born in Dublin in 1772 son of an affluent ironmonger active in local politics. He was educated at a common school and then at a classical academy but when he was about ten he and his elder brother, Benjamin, left the house of their mother's second husband (their father having previously died) and walked to Dublin from Drogheda where they were taken in by their grandfather. John became apprenticed to a soap boiler before the two brothers then moved to London and for a while lived off their father's inheritance. Benjamin set up business as a plumber with John as his assistant. It was when John made the acquaintance of Francis Place that he joined the London Corresponding Society where he quickly became an influential member. When he became involved with two other notable radicals, William Wright and the previously mentioned

John Gale Jones, they tried to manage debating rooms of their own in the Strand. Early in 1796 in an attempt to revitalize the radical movement the LCS resolved to send delegates into the provinces to encourage similar societies. It was whilst addressing a meeting in Birmingham that Binns and Gale Jones were arrested, but it was over a year before they were brought to trial during which time Binns returned to Ireland.

After his acquittal Binns and his brother became involved with 'United Britons' which linked extremist English radicals and Irish revolutionaries. It's possible that the two brothers were deeply implicated in a conspiracy with the attempts of the United Irishmen to enlist French military assistance. They were closely associated with both Arthur O'Connor, editor of 'The Press' which was the semi-official paper of the United Irishmen and Father James Coigley, a Catholic Priest who acted as an emissary from the United Irishmen to both France and the United Englishmen. In 1798 John Binns travelled to Kent trying to arrange passage to France for Coigley and O'Connor, but they were all arrested in Margate together with their two servants. Charged with high treason the five were imprisoned in the Tower of London before being tried at the assizes held in Maidstone. However, leading members of the parliamentary opposition testified on O'Connor's behalf and the government was reluctant to reveal the source of secret information on the United Irishmen. Except for Coigley, all were acquitted. When arrested Coigley had been found with incriminating evidence in his pocket and was executed. Binns decided to keep a low profile for a while staying with friends in Derbyshire and Nottinghamshire; during this time he used his mother's maiden name of Pemberton. Towards the end of 1798 he returned to London and went to work for a blacksmith in St. Pancras. The following year the government launched another attack on prominent radicals. It was reported in the press on 19th April,

1799 that John Binns of democratic notoriety and another person by the name of Belton were apprehended by a warrant from the Duke of Portland (Home Secretary) and charged with others in matters of a treasonable nature. Binns, seeing the officer approach, endeavoured to make his escape across the fields but was pursued and captured. Upon his lodgings being searched a variety of papers were found and he was taken into custody along with several other members of the LCS.

William Longsdon had unearthed some very disturbing and controversial information about a man, although they hadn't met, he knew he didn't like. He just could not comprehend why Sarah would have been involved in such things. To his immense relief what he then discovered completely altered the picture he had reluctantly been forming of her. John Binns left England for the United States in 1801 and hadn't been seen this side of the Atlantic since then. So the wretched man had gone from these shores and furthermore it couldn't possibly be the John Binns associated with Sarah Gardom who had written to his mother. Thank goodness for that!

So who was John Binns, of Windsor Terrace, how had he known Sarah and what had she been doing in London? His discoveries of the other John Binns had given William cause for thought and to question whether Sarah's circumstances prompted her to have radical sympathies and desires for social reform. He reflected on the fact that he, William Longsdon, was privileged, had been born into the gentry, a long established Derbyshire family, although granted, he worked very hard to maintain his station in life. Furthermore, he knew that his family, even more so his mother's family, the Gardoms, had prospered through not only hard work and risk taking but by employment of cheap labour, often children, in the quarries, the lead mines and the cotton mills.

# CHAPTER FIVE

**William Longsdon visits Mr Binns, gentleman.**

William had taken a room at the newly rebuilt Post House, known as the Angel Inn, which advertised itself as a hotel for gentlemen and their families. The coach drew up outside the brick built four storey building with symmetrically placed bow and sash windows.  As always when he visited the Capital he was conscious of the noise, dirt, appalling smell and the bustling about of people in the street, even at that hour in the morning. It was 7 am as William had taken the mail coach from Derby, travelling through the night. Once inside he was soon shown to a pleasant, light, airy and spacious room on the second floor, the windows affording good views of the surrounding area where substantial rebuilding was taking place. He was glad not to be accommodated near the large first floor assembly room which served as a centre for public administration and meetings. The journey had been fast – about thirteen or fourteen hours – on the macadamised roads – and they had made several stops to drop and pick up mail as well as change horses at various coaching inns along the route. He decided to get some sleep and freshen up before his appointment at mid-day. He was one of those fortunate people who could take a nap at any time and awaken feeling completely refreshed; this ability had helped him enormously with all his foreign travels.

The reason for his visit to London was two-fold; he was meeting his agent, Vernon Grove, at Rules in Covent Garden to discuss various business deals and, as was their custom, they would sit in one of the booths of the oak panelled restaurant where they could talk without being overheard. William was always fascinated by the way Vernon's little finger bent in a lady-like way as he raised his wine glass, but it wasn't an affectation; it was a permanent feature of his anatomy. He could happily eat beef suet pudding followed by yet more suet pastry, usually apple dumplings or roly-poly pudding. And the tall, silver haired dignified gentleman with impeccable manners never seemed to suffer from indigestion or gain an ounce in weight (at home Mrs Grove must have rigorously watched his diet) whereas William had to watch his waistline very carefully. In any case, he was a widower and he might still yet meet a lady to tickle his fancy!

Situated near a tollgate on the Great North Road the old building of The Angel was now replaced and was a regular refuge for travellers entering London from the north and with extensive lodging for livestock traders having large fields nearby to rest their animals before the onward journey to Smithfield meat market. The Inn had originally been a large three storey building with enclosed stable buildings alongside and a quadrangle courtyard with galleried interior where, as the first staging coach inn outside the City of London, visitors would have arrived to the scene of not just drinking, but tradesmen selling their wares, play enacting and even court sessions with much heckling and rowdiness. The Angel also accommodated long distance coaches, to some extent, for those who chose not to arrive in The City after dark as the open land between Islington and The City itself was dangerous to cross due to the risk of vagrants, rogues, imposter soldiers or highwaymen relieving people of their valuables or even their lives. But times had changed.

\*\*\*

"Stop, stop, stop" Mr Binns gesticulated wildly in his theatrical effort to inform William of the reason for his visit. William was now comfortably seated in the room at the front of the smart house, in the Plain English style, at the end of Windsor Terrace, just off the City Road and not far from The Angel Inn. The main entrance at the side of the property was through wide gates with a good turning place, space for several carriages and a coach house at the rear of the courtyard. They were in the beautifully panelled drawing room (tapestries were by then out of fashion but still needed in cold and draughty places like Little Longstone Manor) and the big sash windows allowed plenty of light into the room. In elaborate alcoves were beautiful blue and white jars, probably brought to Europe by the Dutch and East India Companies and William admired the mahogany furniture. Foreign furniture and art dealers were amazed at the opportunities in England and often 'fleeced' the English – selling for greater sums what they had imported for a trifle from France and Italy. He was listening to the drama played out for his benefit.

"Stop the carriage. That poor woman has been knocked into the road by a vagrant who's gone running off." Mr Binns said he quickly alighted from the vehicle and rushed to the aid of the woman who was trying to get up out of the mud and muck of the badly rutted road. He offered to help the distressed young lady, her dress torn and mud splattered, but fortunately it transpired that she was uninjured. She told him she had been robbed of the parcel she was carrying and she gladly accepted his offer to take her back to Burlington House in Piccadilly - now without the wig she had been to collect for her employer. Yes, she agreed it had been foolish to walk alone in that particular area and would not do so in future; there was no need to as there was always a carriage at her disposal. Neither she nor Mr Binns could guess what her assailant would do with the article. It had been wrapped in brown paper but he would no doubt find a buyer for the surprise contents. Mr Binns insisted on reporting the matter to the law and agreed to be a witness in the matter, besides which, he found the dainty young lady with her wide eyes and pretty turned up nose, very becoming and wanted to see her again. (Whilst assisting her he had unashamedly glimpsed sight of her trim ankles). Mr Binns explained to William that the unfortunate incident was the start of his acquaintance and then, eventually, friendship with Sarah.

So William learnt that Sarah had been in service to someone in Piccadilly. Who was it?

Mr Binns wanted to continue with his story - which he did during a very pleasant dinner served by his housekeeper and a maid. Having eaten a hearty breakfast and then lunch with Vernon, William was not very hungry. Thank goodness he had refrained from choosing anything too substantial at Rules – the waiter had served him with a look of disdain – "only oysters, sir?" However, he had succumbed to a light custard confection. But now, sat at Mr Binns table, the first delicious course consisted of a white fish with an oyster sauce (more oysters, but he loved them) then followed by a ragout (he guessed it was mutton) made, he was enlightened, to a French recipe. For dessert there was a selection of raisins, walnuts and almonds and a glass of Madeira wine. Perfect. William thought this was a very agreeable life, so far removed from the wilds of Derbyshire, although he wondered if he could tolerate for too long the streets of filth and poverty outside these four walls. William could hear from the hall the chiming of the tall, beautiful enamel faced grandfather clock; he had covetously noticed it on his arrival but had immediately realized that the ceilings at home were too low to accommodate such a beautiful object. He returned his attention to Mr Binns.

The proceedings were at The Old Bailey early in 1789 and it was recorded that Jasper Lee was indicted for assault and robbery and feloniously stealing a gentleman's powdered wig. Being a gentleman and a confident, reliable witness Mr Binns had no trouble in convincing the jury that the accused was guilty. Legal representation for either side was barely necessary as it was such a clear cut case. Lee was sentenced to death by hanging. Sarah was horrified at the outcome; during her three years in London she had not encountered such ruthlessness. She had witnessed, whilst in the spectators gallery, the previous case of Mary Acton convicted of stealing 10 suckling pigs which resulted in a sentence of seven years in goal. Sometime later when they had reason to speak of the court case, Mr Binns told Sarah that Mary Acton was transported along with about 250 other female convicts - some who had already been in goal for two or three years - on the fleet ship Lady Juliana which left Plymouth in July of that year. The route went via Tenerife, St Jago and Rio de Janeiro and finally arrived at Port Jackson, Australia after a voyage of over ten months during which many convicts must have died.

William wanted to know where Sarah was in service and Mr Binns promised to take him the next day.

*** 

Mr Binns would not allow William to walk the short distance to his house in Windsor Terrace and so met him with his smart horse drawn phaeton at The Angel for their drive to Piccadilly but first making a detour to an establishment in Threadneedle Street where he delivered some papers wrapped in brown paper, secured with string and sealing wax. William noticed the brass plate strategically placed at the side of the entrance door – 'Sutcliffe and Binns, Ship and Insurance Brokers'.

Without having to ask such an ungentlemanly question as to his profession, William had learnt the nature of Mr Binns occupation. No wonder he had an air of success and affluence about him. They continued their journey. Such an interesting name: Threadneedle Street and they pondered on its derivation. Was it from the Anglo-Saxon word meaning "to prosper" or was it from a signboard showing three needles being the arms of needle-makers who had premises in the street? Or was it related to the Worshipful Company of Merchant Taylors (threads and needles) as the livery company's hall had been situated on Threadneedle Street since 1347? Or was it simply that children played a game 'thread the needle' there? Mr Binns pointed out The Bank of England known as the 'Old Lady of Threadneedle Street' and the imposing London Stock Exchange. It was within the domed rotunda that served for many years as the market place for the buying and selling of stocks. At about the same time of 1734 The Baltic Exchange was founded in the Virginia and Baltic Coffee House and the headquarters of the South Sea Company were also located on the street. Originally, some of the buildings had been shops, banks, inns, offices, and coffee houses.

William had never previously had time to explore much of London as he had always been on a tight schedule, so, as they travelled Mr Binns told him as much as he could about the area. Their route took them along Holborn which seemed to be full of bad tempered coach drivers in a hurry with their big hackney carriages and landaus, wielding their whips and swearing at their horses or anybody who got in the way. From there they crossed to Piccadilly via Shaftesbury Avenue. It was so busy, teeming with people of every race, horses and carriages and carts. William could hear a cacophony of sounds - the bells from church steeples, postmen ringing bells, street organs, cries of street vendors, music from itinerant musicians and he caught a whiff of the hot potatoes and other food being sold on street corners. He could barely see the buildings properly, many of them theatres where Mr Binns was telling him that he had taken Sarah on many occasions. When they reached Piccadilly Mr Binns pointed out Burlington House, a very grand colonnaded Palladian mansion. William wished they could stop but it was so busy and they didn't really have time as Mr Binns had other plans in mind; he wanted to carry on to another property in the city where Sarah and her employers had eventually moved to.

"I will show you" he had said seeing how disappointed William looked. "It is in Cavendish Square."

They were driving up Regent Street where life seemed to be at a more leisurely pace; William could see fashionably dressed ladies shopping. They approached Cavendish Square from the old Roman road of Oxford Street, still, even after its name change sometimes referred to as Tyburn Road. In the year 1715 the plan for building Cavendish Square and several other streets north of Oxford Street had been mooted. Two years later the ground was laid out with a circular plantation in the centre enclosed, planted and surrounded by a low wall and wooden railings. The buildings made slow progress and it was several years before the square and the surrounding streets were completed. It was recorded that in 1739 in St Marylebone there were nearly six hundred houses but by the year 1806 there were nearly nine thousand with a corresponding increase in the number of horse-drawn coaches and a population of six hundred thousand. Because of The South Sea Bubble in the year 1720 building stopped for a while and many buildings remained in an incomplete state. William realised that Cavendish Square and surrounding streets were named after the various relatives of Robert Harley closely connected with his own neighbours The

Dukes of Devonshire and The Dukes of Portland who owned estates in Derbyshire. From Oxford Street, through a few small streets they arrived in the south-western corner of the square and via Vere Street proceeded to make their way northward. Mr Binns pointed out Oxford Chapel where the second Duke of Portland married Lady Margaret Harley the heiress of Lord Oxford. They crossed Henrietta Street, where at number three resided the Countess of Mornington, mother of The Duke of Wellington and William glimpsed fine houses in Bentinck Street and next Wigmore Street from where they passed into Cavendish Square. His first impression was of lovely, spacious parkland and beautiful trees but William was surprised by the size of the properties where so many rich and famous people lived: the biggest he had seen in Derbyshire were Hardwick Hall, Chatsworth House and lovely old Haddon Hall which had been empty for some years. He had never seen in one area so many huge mansions set in their own grounds; such displays of wealth and opulence. Eventually they slowed down outside the huge and dreary looking mansion called Harcourt House which occupied the centre of the west side of the square and Mr Binns explained that it was the town residence of the Duke of Portland. The house featured a large courtyard facing the square and an imposing covered carriage porch (ports cochere) through which a horse and carriage could pass in order for the occupants to alight under cover, protected from the weather. The large garden was planted with wide-spreading trees and William could see huge stable buildings at the back. Mr Binns said that this was all highly unusual in London when it was built in the 1720's, but its monastic appearance was referred to as more like a convent than a house for a man of quality! Burlington House in Piccadilly looked far superior.

It had been revealed to him where she had worked and lived but now William was assembling a few thoughts about her circumstances as to how or why she had come to be in London. He was about to ask Mr Binns the nature of Sarah's occupation when his kind host said

"We need to go to Clipstone Street. That is to where Sarah eventually moved when she left Harcourt House. William, I have so much to tell you and there is so much I don't know."

"Perhaps" replied William "we can try and piece it together between us."

In a matter of minutes they were out of Cavendish Square and into the beautiful wide street called Portland Place. Its two rows of stately homes were designed by Robert Adam and named after the ground landlord. William thought the spaciousness of the area could afford some trees. They were soon heading into a completely different scene. Mr Binns explained that the neighbourhood of Great Portland Street, towards the upper end, was mostly the home of artists and sculptors as was Clipstone Street; these properties were also owned by The Duke of Portland. In this fascinating area of creative activity there were artists in their studios attempting to paint masterpieces, picture framers in their workshops making and carefully gilding the frames and artisans chipping away at their stone or marble in the yards behind or beneath their houses. William briefly thought of Chatsworth House when his ancestor, the talented blacksmith John Gardom, worked amongst the artists and artisans during the rebuilding of the Duke of Devonshire's stately home more than a hundred years previously. He guessed that many of them, including those who had come from Europe with William of Orange, had probably settled here in Clipstone Street where they would be conveniently placed to take advantage of the opportunities associated with new building works for an affluent society in fashionable London.

Mr Binns pointed out a well-proportioned terraced house where they slowed down outside for a few minutes.

"This is where Sarah lived in comfortable rooms for the last years of her life. I often visited her here. She said she was free now and she was happy. She enjoyed little outings to the theatre, she conducted herself like a lady of quality and I enjoyed her company. She was a good cook. Her hand writing was beautiful and she could illuminate it with coloured inks and paints; quite exquisite. I miss her." William wondered what Sarah had meant by saying that she was 'free now.'

"William," said Mr Binns, "we need to visit the solicitor - can you stay another day?"

Later that day at The Angel the two men, served by a buxom wench showing too much bosom, ate a hearty dinner of good roast beef, and plenty of it, helped down with the landlord's best ale. They talked well into the night. Mr Binns told William that when he first met Sarah when she had been robbed and the ensuing court case he thought there was a mutual attraction between them but she did not encourage a close friendship. Eventually he married Elsie, who, sadly died in childbirth along with their baby. Afterwards he enjoyed a few dalliances, but none of those ladies inspired in him a desire to settle down.

"Then I saw her. It was not until many years later at The Frost Fair; must have been 1814 when the Thames had frozen over and there was a party atmosphere on the ice. Not only were there ice skating races and performances but from tents and stalls tradesmen were offering their services such as letter press printing, others selling their wares, there was gin and rum if you fancied it, there were bookstalls, games such as skittles and would you believe it, a casino offering roulette and a wheel of fortune. Meat was spit-roasted and slices sold for extortionate prices. And there she was with a group of people. Despite beautiful furs keeping out the cold and almost hiding her pretty face I'd have known her anywhere; that little turned up nose and wide eyes. Oh, I can tell you, I was delighted to see her. I asked if I could write to her and she gave me her address: Sarah Green at number seventeen Clipstone Street. I could hardly sleep until I saw her again, and yes, from there our friendship blossomed. I felt intoxicated by her and I suppose we should have married but it didn't seem important as we both, by then, were in our early fifties." Mr Binns was interrupted by his attentive friend

"What do you mean, Sarah Green?"

"That was the name I had always known" was the reply. "Some years later during supper at her house Sarah said she had something to tell me, that her name was Sarah Gardom but she offered no explanation as to why she had deceived me. Yes, I felt temporarily deluded and hurt but I had to respect her reticence. I knew little of her life, or she of mine for that matter, so I came to terms with it. She was such fun to be with, she had made no demands on me and I thought maybe one day she would tell me. Those fifteen years we spent together seemed to fly by and in the summer of 1829 Sarah's health deteriorated and she asked me to write to your mother after her death, which I did. When I went to the Notary Public, as requested, and verified the handwriting of her will I made a huge discovery. I could not help but read the small document in which she bequeathed her silver watch to Miss Sarah Gardom daughter of Mr John Gardom of Bolsover and the residue of her estate to the said Mr John Gardom. It was a shock, I must say. She had never mentioned any relatives."

"John Gardom is her son" said William. "My father saw him in the market in Bolsover a few years ago. How incredible that Sarah kept silent about him for all these years."

William agreed to collect, the next day, the few bequeathed, precious items and small paintings from the executor, solicitor George Peters, in Penton Place. After his return home and making sure that his family and affairs were in order he would deliver the items to John Gardom in Bolsover; the solicitor had already written to John informing him of his inheritance.

So it was established that Sarah had been employed by the Portland family and that both she and her illegitimate son were, or had been, living in properties belonging to the Duke of Portland. Was that just a coincidence or was there more to it than that? Why had Sarah been so secretive about her past? Had her son known of her existence - probably not as she went under the name of Green and not Gardom? Sarah seemed to have been totally estranged from her family. How had her parents and siblings explained her disappearance? Perhaps they had no contact with John either. Even to William, a man of the world, it all seemed very sad. And because he had been committed to a very busy life abroad for some years he had not given much thought to his mother's relatives in Baslow and Edensor.

William promised to enlighten Mr Binns of whatever discoveries he made and both men hoped to meet again, probably in Derbyshire, in due course.

# CHAPTER SIX

## William returns from London

Having heaved his portmanteau into the carriage he squeezed himself into the remaining small space between the other three travellers. He guessed they would reach their destinations before the end of the journey to Derby and he hoped they wouldn't talk too much as he was tired. The main old Roman road out of London was Watling Street and the first few hours seemed to pass quickly, without incident, but gave William time to reflect on his life.

At forty years of age he'd weathered quite a few experiences. After only being married for a year his first wife and their daughter had both died in childbirth. He had been distraught and his mother had taken him one day to Gardom Edge. They had chosen a bright clear day for their ride through Baslow, over the river and up the steep Chesterfield road. When they turned left off the road their horses picked their way very carefully up along the stony, meandering track through the bracken and broken branches of wind damaged trees. The hefted flock of bedraggled sheep fled in all directions to make way for them and they could hear the mewing sounds of the buzzards circling above. William and his mother dismounted when they could ride no higher. The far reaching views were amazing, they seemed to be up in the billowing white clouds, almost in heaven and she left his side for a while to leave him with his own thoughts. It was a place of peace and tranquillity - ethereal. He did not know how long he sat there on a rocky ledge but when she eventually rejoined him she showed him the quarried workings of the escarpment where once men, women and children had toiled, cutting out millstones, water troughs and stone gateposts. And they looked down at the farm of their ancestors below where some of the Gardom relatives still lived and worked. Over the years he had returned to the edge and found the solace which he sought when his life had seemed so desolate.

Two years after the loss of his first wife and baby he had married Hannah Goodwin and they had three children, Elizabeth Ann was now ten, Charles was five and Emma, who had been born in Charleston, South Carolina whilst he had been working there, was three. But he couldn't bear to think about it.

He was looking forward to seeing his children; it was only a few days that he had been away in London but it felt much longer. He was especially looking forward to seeing his unmarried sister, Lizzy who was at home with the children at Little Longstone Manor; he knew that she would be very interested to hear about his visit to see Mr Binns. It occurred to him that he took his sister for granted; she had stepped in when tragedy had blighted his life once again. He resolved to be more appreciative of her; a little gift of jewellery now and again would not go amiss. Perhaps he should have stopped in Regent Street instead of just hurriedly purchasing a few trinkets from the tradesmen near The Angel. And wherever he had travelled he had looked forward to the comfort of his own bed, though, with no one to share it with these days.

After the first stop to exchange mail and horses at The White Horse in Redbourn at 10.30pm William managed to get some sleep propped up by the portly gentleman next to him who shared the journey for the whole route, although who periodically awoke from his slumbers with a loud snort and promptly went back to sleep. The journey by mail coach was interesting for William. As dawn broke he could see that wherever they travelled the landscape had taken on a new appearance brought about by the Agrarian Revolution; hundreds of acres of open waste land and old woodland had been enclosed for arable use. Even the highway men had disappeared from the now macadamised roads since the bushy scrubland and thickets, where once they had lurked, had been ploughed up. It was well known that the new orderly plantations were guarded by game keepers and terrifyingly dangerous man-traps and spring guns. Squires and peasants with small acreages had been bought out to make room for the new scheme; the open fields in the Midlands where once corn had always grown were now enclosed into patch-work patterns of fenced fields where a variety of crops were grown in rotation which meant the soil did not become impoverished.

"Doesn't it look attractive" his portly travelling companion was now awake. The other passengers had already alighted. "Are you a land owner?" he queried.

"Indeed I am" replied William thinking that his country attire had revealed his occupation. "For as long as I can remember our fields at home have always had stone walled boundaries which afford shelter and protection to the sheep during our harsh weather. Sometimes in the Peak district it has taken many, many years to clear the land of stone to make it worthy of cultivation or for better grazing. There's a farm beyond the top of Gardom Edge near my home where it has taken the owners a hundred years to move all the stone off the fields to build their house, buildings and boundary walls."

"Well I never" said the man. "I'm in the legal profession in the City, Ptomoly Hogg by name, and have little knowledge of farming."

"Pleased to meet you; I'm William Longsdon" he replied as they shook hands and made themselves more comfortable in the extra space vacated by the other travellers. Having slept a little William was happy to talk and told him he knew that not only in Derbyshire, but everywhere in the country, the larger land owners were consolidating their estates and new farming methods were being employed. The population in England's past had been scantily scattered and was, broadly speaking, self-sufficient. There had been few large towns and three quarters of the people lived mainly on the land and by the land. Every farm and cottage had its own spinning wheel and many had their own hand-loom. There had been no difference in labour - the farmers were manufacturers; the manufacturers were farmers. There had been no problem with the distribution of wealth because the economy had worked. Wages had been eked out by spinning, weaving, keeping fowls and geese and maybe a cow that roamed the common and pigs that subsided in the woods. Wages had been less of a problem under the old system but since the revolutionary changes in farming there were big land owners, capitalist farmers and the landless labourers had to be paid wages. Throughout the land there were now better roads, canals and machines diverting cottage and village industry to town factories resulting in denying the peasant family from spinning and other small manufacturing activities whereby they had struggled to achieve a meagre living. Yes, for better or worse, his family having been involved in the cotton manufacturing industry had helped to galvanize this change.

"I can tell you" said Mr Hogg "that Private Acts of Parliament were passed which overrode the resistance of individual owners to enclosure and each had to accept the compensation money or land awarded by Parliamentary Commissioners whose decisions were backed by law. Batches of these revolutionary

Acts were rushed through every parliament of the King (George III). Shocking really; this was fundamental change for the benefit of the rich, often at the expense of the poor. But how does all this progress affect you?"

William said he was considering how he could improve his farming methods. The age of enclosure had also brought about improvements in draining the land, drilling, sowing, manure-spreading, breeding and feeding livestock - not just improving roads and rebuilding farm premises. Such were the improvements of land culture and the introduction of new crops, such as turnips, that he was led to believe incomes could increase almost tenfold for landowners and their tenants. On this journey he had seen with his own eyes how the once vast cornfields where the cattle used to stray among the stubble in search of food were now enclosed in moderate sized fields divided by hawthorn hedges, wherein beasts could be pastured on good grass. At the same time much more of the arable land was used for raising crops such as different grass strains and roots to feed cattle and sheep through winter. The net result was a bigger increase in the amount of corn produced for bread and beer and even greater increase in the numbers and size of animals. If William could achieve this it meant that instead of slaughtering stock at the end of autumn because there was no winter feed, with good management and better buildings they could be overwintered. That would put an end to poorly fleshed salted meat; it could be replaced with fresh beef and mutton of a better quality at varying times. Better food meant better health. Scurvy and other skin diseases, not just restricted to the poor, would grow out.

By now they were in Derby, in need of breakfast and hopefully, for William, one of his farm hands would be at the market place with the gig to take him back home, with luck and barring any accidents, by early afternoon.  William was not surprised when his portly travelling companion said he had been recommended a good place where they would be well fed and gladly agreed to accompany him.

William was soon greeted by his three children when he arrived home; they had heard the horse and carriage coming along the lane as they eagerly awaited his return.

"Papa, papa have you brought us presents" they chorused as they draped themselves all over him.

"Let me get my breath back first" he exclaimed "and do quieten down or I'll go back to London.  Now, let me change out of these clothes and I'll see what I've got for you. But first I need to know from your Aunt Lizzie if you've all been good children."

"Yes, we have" they all shouted "yes, yes, yes."

# CHAPTER SEVEN

# CHAPTER SEVEN

**William goes to Bolsover**

William opened the package and extracted the ladies silver fob watch. It was stunning being heart shaped to the front and with a highly decorative face in gold gilt and set with two little rubies. The round silver case was ornately decorated in a foliate design and with a decoratively patterned back. He pressed down the nob on top and the back sprung open to reveal the engraved inscription:

*Sarah*

*For All You Are To Me*

*W*

He set the time by the mantel clock and wound it up and to his surprise the beautiful little object started to tick.

"Lizzie, where are you? Look at this."

He found his sister upstairs trying to sort out the contents of the linen room.

"Oh, how exquisite – I wonder who 'W' was."

He put the time-piece back into the package and carefully rewrapped all the items for John Gardom.

\*\*\*

Having made sure that all his Estate affairs were in order, that his sister and the children were well, that the farm was running smoothly under the competent management of Mr Bates, it did not take William long to visit John Gardom in Bolsover, a distance of about twenty three miles. He set off at dawn, the precious items safely packed into a large leather satchel strapped to his back. Just as he was about to depart his sister appeared.

"Thank you for getting my boots cleaned, Lizzie."

"Don't go for a minute" she said. "Here, wear this. It's Father's old coat, bigger than yours. I know you'll look like a hunchback but wear it over the satchel so it won't be so conspicuous and don't pull your hat down so your ears stick out like that; you look totally queer in the attic!" He knew she meant well, but in fact she was right. He was going alone and the last thing he wanted was to be robbed.

He hoped he would be able to find a comfortable bed and stabling for his horse in the best hostelry that Bolsover had to offer; it was probably too far to return home the same day. Fortunately, he had a safe journey using the well-worn green roads. He came across a few itinerants being moved on from place to place and skirted them widely and he was held up for a short time whilst a shepherd rounded up some stray sheep with his yapping dog. At least it gave him time to dismount, obey a call of nature, stretch his legs and let his horse graze the grass verge. The solicitor, George Peters, had furnished him with the address in Bolsover which was easily located. The farmhouse was well situated on high ground with its land falling away to the rear and well protected from the elements. There were a few small farm buildings easily accessible from the road. Feeling tired and dirty William was not met with an over-enthusiastic reception from John and his wife Margaret. They were courteous enough but although Mr Peters, the solicitor, had already informed them about the will of Sarah Gardom, John seemed almost speechless with shock. He managed to convey to William that he had been brought up as an orphan and found it hard to believe that his mother had been alive for all this time. He was unable to speak about the matter, for the time being at least. Although William thought that they could easily have offered him a bed for the night and shelter for his horse he was not offended; he tried to imagine how he would feel in those circumstances. He had handed over the packages but before leaving said that he hoped to see them before too long and perhaps they would eventually like to visit him in Little Longstone.

\*\*\*

"Yes, we can find you a bed and a decent plate of food, squire. Never busy on a Tuesday not being a market day. Nice horse you've got there – don't see many like that; he'll be quite happy here. We've been stabling horses for years. Come far have you?"

William easily found a table in the corner of the tap room as the place was almost empty and he hoped it wasn't a sign of poorly kept ale and bad food. Oh well, he was here now and would have to make the best of things. He quickly downed the first pint and was half way through his second when the landlord's wife appeared with a steaming hot plate of game stew and herby dumplings. There had been no choice but it smelt pretty good. Then she brought him a huge dish of potatoes. When he expressed surprise at the quantity of food she said the farmers round there had got hearty appetites.

"Anyway, you get it down you young man - looks like you need a bit of flesh on your bones!"

William thought she'd returned to the kitchen but after a little while she came back to his table with another tankard of ale.

"This is on the house" she said. "Come far have you?" She plonked herself down on the chair opposite him. "Don't mind if I take the weight off my feet do you?"

William obviously didn't have any choice.

"I live near Baslow, not that far."

"Here on business are you? Got a nice little family, have you?"

"Um, yes, three young children."

"Wife?"

William's face must have clouded over for she said "Oh, sorry. You look sad. What's happened? Do you want to talk about it?"

"I suppose it would do me good. I can't keep trying to shut things out of my mind."

It turned out her name was Jessie and he told her about his first exciting voyage to South Carolina with his brother John. He explained that his brother had already been to Nova Scotia but despite the war between America and Great Britain in 1815, which hampered progress with most things for a period, thankfully ship building had improved since John's sea voyage on the packet ship.

"I've never been anywhere" she said.

"We arrived under sail into the harbour of Charleston in the Atlantic Ocean and our first view was a very picturesque city. Its spires and public buildings seemed to rise out of the sea, whilst the richness of the surrounding foliage made the place look particularly attractive. We soon discovered that the streets were well laid out but the assortment of colourful buildings had little uniformity and we thought there was a need for public squares and spaces, however, the houses and various other buildings were surrounded by spacious grounds with numerous trees of all kinds giving the city a pretty appearance. It was such a contrast from our home in the Derbyshire Peaks! Of course, we had gone there because Charleston was one of the leading commercial cities of the South, being the outlet for a very rich rice and cotton producing country and a point of supply for an extensive territory embracing North Carolina, Georgia, Alabama, Florida, Tennessee and Mississippi."

"My guess is that you were interested in the cotton" ventured Jessie.

"Yes, completely accurate. We wanted to make fustian."

"Whatever is that, I've never heard of it?"

"I expect you know it really. It's a kind of coarse twilled cotton cloth, like hard wearing corduroy.

The history of the city interested us - at least it did have a history - especially as it was founded in 1670 as Charles Towne in honour of King Charles II of England. After Charles was restored to the English throne following Oliver Cromwell's Protectorate, he granted the charter Province of Carolina to eight of his friends who were known as Lord Proprietors. It took seven years before the group arranged for settlement expeditions; the first of these founded Charles Towne. The community was established by several shiploads of settlers from Bermuda under the governor William Sayle. Other first settlers primarily came from England and Barbados as well as Bermuda and among these were 'free people of colour' established in the West Indies where racial demarcations were less rigid in the early colonial years. They were of partial African and European descent; people who were not enslaved. Charles Towne attracted a mixture of ethnic and religious groups although, because of the battles between English Royalty and the Roman Catholic Church, practising Catholics could not settle there. Africans were brought to the City on the middle passage, first as servants, then as slaves, in fact it was the main dropping off point for Africans captured and transported to the English-American colonies for sale as slaves."

"They say there were Black slaves at the castle here years ago, at any rate, pretty boys working in the stables" interrupted Jessie.

William continued for at least he knew she was listening.

"In the port physicians inspected incoming ships to protect the settlement from contagious diseases; passengers on ships suspected of carrying infection were isolated. Africans and white passengers arriving from Europe or other American colonies were quarantined, being isolated aboard ship, in homes or in pest houses known as lazaretts. Africans were held the shortest time because they were to be auctioned and at times slave ship captains managed to evade quarantine altogether.

But by the time we arrived in the wealthy city it was a bustling trade-centre, the hub of Atlantic trade for the southern colonies, its early success based on the trade of deer skin hides which were used to make pantaloons for men, gloves and book bindings. We had a wonderful time buying gifts for the family back home. There was so much to explore and discover that we sometimes forgot why we were there!

Landowners had experimented with cash-crops such as tea and silk. African slaves had brought with them knowledge of rice cultivation which the land-owners made into successful businesses. African slaves from the Caribbean had also brought with them the skills to grow and use the indigo plant, a rare commodity which produced a luxurious colour and with supporting subsidies from Britain it became a leading export for the landowners. Not only had Charles Towne grown but the community's cultural and social opportunities had developed, especially for the elite merchants and planters."

"Anybody serving in this place?" A jovial looking character had already reached down his pewter tankard from above the counter. He was obviously a regular.

"Oh, serve yourself George. Can't you see I'm tied up at the moment" replied Jessie.

"I see, you've got someone better have you…..deserted me have you?"

"Don't worry" said Jessie to William "It's only my brother…. comes in this time every night."

William was pleased she was so interested and thought she must have been bored with the usual customers.

"The relationship between Britain and the colonists had deteriorated and Charles Towne was twice the target of British attacks by Sir Henry Clinton during the American Revolution. After a long siege American General Benjamin Lincoln surrendered his entire force; it was the biggest defeat of the war. The British retained control for a couple of years and then left whereupon the city's name was officially changed to Charleston. Despite everything the city became even more prosperous with its plantation-dominated economy. The invention of the cotton-gin (a machine for separating the seeds from the raw cotton) revolutionised the production of the crop and it quickly became South Carolina's major export commodity. Needless to say the plantations relied heavily on slave labour and slaves were also the main work force within the city working as domestics, artisans, market workers and labourers. Eventually, years of oppression and inequality erupted in a massive slave revolt in 1822, resulting in thirty five of them being hanged. By the time my daughter Emma Jane was born there in 1827 the slave trade had been officially abolished."

"So, your wife had joined you?"

"Yes, once we'd set up our company and John returned home, Hannah and my two oldest children joined me. I found a pretty little house in a quiet street for us to rent. It was away from all the troubled areas; there were still unresolved problems with the majority of the labour force."

William stopped talking. He wanted to remember the happy few years when his wife and children had joined him in Charleston.

Jessie put a hand over his in a comforting gesture. "Do go on" she said.

He took another swig of his ale and wondered why he was telling a stranger all this. Choking on his words and almost in a whisper he said

"She died. Hannah. The pain of it all, her illness, her death, the loss of a wife and mother to my children is still just too much to dwell on."

Jessie patted his hand again. "You'll feel better now... now that you've talked about it, got it off your chest. I'll get you some fruit pie."

Later he considered the fact that Lizzie too was suffering. They had lost both their parents and two brothers in a short space of time, but he could see that she had channelled her energies into caring for his children. It was time to pull himself together.

*** 

On his return William wrote to Mr Peters informing him that the mission had been accomplished and he wrote to Mr Binns telling him of the visit to Bolsover and that he was not very happy with the outcome so far, especially as he had gone to such a lot of time and trouble. However, there was little he could do about the situation and hoped that, given time, there would be a favourable outcome.

John Gardom had been brought up as an orphan (William did not know where) and in ignorance of his parentage. When, hopefully, the time came to meet John at least William and Mr Binns would be able to tell him something about his mother. William decided that he would find out as much as possible about the residents of Harcourt House, the Portland family.

# CHAPTER EIGHT

## Dukes of Portland

A black face stared down at him from the roof. William had been to see the farm bailiff about various estate matters and then Jack Bates as he wanted to discuss new farming policies and was surprised to see him on top of his roof with a stiff, sweep's brush cleaning the chimney; at least he assumed it was Jack!

"Got rooks making a mess; the missus is complaining" he shouted down. "See we could do with a bit of repair work as well" as he pointed in the direction of two of the nearby buildings.

There was always repair and maintenance work to be done, not just on the manor house and farm buildings, but all the estate cottages too. William really did need to make the estate more efficient and profitable in order to sustain continuity for his family, employees and tenants.

\*\*\*

"You'll never guess, William - we've had an invitation" said Lizzie before he'd even had time to take his coat off.

"Well, I can't guess and I won't know if you don't tell me and why are you so excited dear sister? We've had invitations before."

"The Eyres have invited us to Dinner at Hassop Hall in two weeks' time. What on earth shall I wear?"

"Goodness me, Lizzie, you are excited, it's not like you. Calm down and tell me what's been happening today and then tell me about dinner at Hassop." They were interrupted by the three youngsters:

"Our new ponies have arrived" they shouted in unison.

"Yes, yes that's good. I know you're excited; I'll come and have a look when I've had time to speak to your Aunt."

\*\*\*

Ann could already ride at the age of ten "Heels down, feet straight and don't stick your bottom out like that" he called to her. Charles, who William had got on a leading reign, was bobbing about like a sack of potatoes on his fat little pony. It was quite amusing. Lizzie lifted Emma up to her father and she sat snuggled into his body with his spare arm around her. This was the first time his excited little daughter had been on horseback. Lizzie took hold of the leading reign and walked round with Charles on the mildly mannered chestnut coloured Shetland; they all walked very steadily around the small paddock.

"I want some jumps, Papa." Ann was looking very confident on her sturdy black fell pony.

"Let's put some up another day" replied her father "just you and me. You need to get used to your pony first and he with you; build up a relationship before you expect too much of him. I expect you to look after him properly too; feeding every day and grooming him before and after riding. And don't forget to look after his feet. Understand? Good."

William had decided that his children couldn't learn to ride too soon and it would do them good to grow up responsibly knowing that they had to take care of their ponies.

\*\*\*

It transpired that the Eyre family from nearby Hassop Hall were having a dinner party for about twenty people. The occasion was most likely to show off their recent alterations and improvements to the front of the house. They had already built a Catholic Church in the severest Classical Revival style which gave it the appearance of an Etruscan temple. There was even an underground passage from the Church to the Hall. Lizzie did her best to enquire about who the other guests might be so that she could brief her brother. The Duke and Duchess of Devonshire were bound to be invited. An old family friend, Lord Derby, now a widower, had been invited to stay for a few days; at least that's what the housekeeper from Hassop had told the wife of the Longsdons' farm manager, Mrs Bates. Staff were always such a good source of information for they could never keep anything to themselves; the girls who worked in the house for Lizzie were always full of tittle-tattle.

∗∗∗

Lizzie had taken the children to visit a cousin in Great Longstone. William carefully closed the door and went to the escritoire at the end of the room; it was his favourite piece of furniture and had been made at great expense for his great grandfather. He took the key from his waistcoat pocket and opened the beautifully inlaid walnut cabinet then carefully lowered the fall-front which acted as a small writing or reading table. The workmanship never ceased to impress him and with another key he opened one of the many little drawers whilst looking around him to make sure that no-one else had crept silently into the drawing room. From one of the secret compartments he extracted a small box which contained his mother's sapphire and diamond drop earrings with matching pear shaped pendant on a heavy gold chain. Yes, they were exactly right. He carefully put them back and locked up the cabinet.

∗∗∗

William was doing his best to find information about the Portland family. His reliable informant, Vernon Grove, who knew everything there was to know about 'anyone who was of note' had sent William a brief family history to keep him satisfied, at least for the time being.

The First Earl of Portland, William Bentinck, who died in 1709 was descended from an ancient and noble family of Gulderland and became page of honour to William, prince of Orange, from which position he advanced to gentleman of the bedchamber. It was in this capacity that he had accompanied William to England in 1670, and along with him was created doctor of civil law by the University of Oxford. Afterwards he became a colonel in a Dutch regiment of guards. When the prince of Orange was afflicted with smallpox, prompted by suggestions of the physicians, Bentinck volunteered to lie in bed with him, that the heat of his body might impede further deterioration and dissipate the disease. ('Goodness gracious' thought William). This remarkable act of self-sacrifice secured him throughout life the special friendship of the prince and by his devotion, prudence and ability fully justified the confidence that was placed in him. In 1677 he was sent by the Prince to England to solicit the hand of Princess Mary, eldest daughter of James (then duke of York). At the Revolution he was the chief means of communication between the Prince and the English nobility and in the delicate negotiations his practical shrewdness greatly eased the arrival of the Prince in England on a proper understanding prior to accepting the Crown. William Bentinck then accompanied William of Orange to England and was made groom of the Privy Purse, first gentleman of the royal bedchamber, and first commissioner of the list of privy councillors. In 1689 he was created Baron Cirencester, Viscount Woodstock and Earl of Portland. During his rank of lieutenant

-general he distinguished himself on many occasions, he had great diplomatic skills but his grave and cold manner rendered him unpopular with the English nobility and his sometimes brusque honesty appeared to make him wanting in respect to the King. His increasing unpopularity eventually caused him to resign his offices and he retired to his property at Bulstrode to enjoy his pursuits of gardening and charity work. When he died his body was interred at Westminster Abbey.

The second Duke of Portland married Lady Margaret Cavendish-Harley who was the richest woman of her time in Great Britain. He was an original governor of the Foundling Hospital in London and was made a Knight of the Garter.

The grandson (1738-1809) of the First Earl of Portland was the Marquess of Titchfield, who was christened William Henry Cavendish-Bentinck and on the death of his father he became the 3rd Duke of Portland in 1762. This is the man who interested William most of all. He was both a British Whig and Tory Statesman, Chancellor of Oxford University and twice Prime Minister of Great Britain, serving first in 1783 and again from 1807 to 1809. The twenty four years between his two terms of Prime Minister was the longest gap between terms of office of anyone in that role. He held every type of title of British nobility - Duke, Marquess, Earl, Viscount and Baron. Being the eldest son of the 2nd Duke of Portland, he inherited many lands from his mother and maternal grandmother. He was educated at Westminster and Christ Church, Oxford and was elected to sit in the Parliament for Weobley in 1761 before entering the Lords when he succeeded his father as Duke of Portland the following year.

***

Lizzie gasped in amazement as they were shown into the palatial high ceilinged dining room at Hassop Hall. The magnificent crystal chandeliers were dancing like a thousand stars reflecting the light from the flickering flames of the elegant tall candles. She had never seen the like before and she was still thinking of how William had surprised and delighted her when he suggested she wore Mother's jewellery with the deep blue satin dress. She had been unaware that the precious items were still in their possession; she thought they had been sold years ago to pay off a debt brought about by one of their father's hare-brained schemes.

When they were being introduced in the drawing room Lizzie had noticed that there was a shortage of women and she had been amused when William had been introduced as Lord Longsdon, a title they no longer used. As they were seated at the beautiful dining table she saw that her brother - probably the youngest man present - was placed next to an elderly gentleman and hoped he wasn't too disappointed not to be next to the most glamorous lady in the party. But she had no need to worry; William had plenty to talk to Lord Derby about and he remembered, as advised by his sister, not to mention the gentleman's first wife who had run off some years ago with John Sackville, Duke of Dorset.

"Yes, my young friend, it was at a party such as this at my estate 'The Oaks' and we were running a sweepstake horse race. The following year my own horse won and we called it the Epsom Oaks. As you can imagine we had a jolly good celebration after my horse, Bridget, won and we proposed a similar race for colts. I tossed a coin with my friend Charles Bunbury for the honour of naming the race." This was always the favourite story of Lord Derby.

"Ah" replied William "I see - that's why it's called the Derby Stakes."

"Tried to get my old friend Portland interested in the horses, but he always had too many other things to occupy him, poor man. Now, mind you his son was a different sort all together; a jolly good man of the turf." That was exactly the cue that William wanted.

"Do you miss your time in Parliament, Sir" queried William who was thinking he must remember to speak to the young lady sat on his other side. Mustn't be bad mannered, perhaps he could continue the conversation with Lord Derby over port when the ladies had withdrawn. And that's precisely what happened.

"I was Chancellor of the Duchy of Lancaster when Portland was selected by Fox and North (the real leaders) to become the head of a coalition government as Prime Minister; the King was with great reluctance compelled to give his assent. It was a difficult time because the government was concerned about the power of the East India Company. Charles Fox attempted to persuade parliament to pass a bill that would replace the company's directors with a board of commissioners but King George made it known that he would consider anyone voting for the Bill as an enemy. As a result of this interference Portland's government resigned and William Pitt became Prime Minister. In this ministry I think Portland served for a short period as First Lord of the Treasury and I'm pretty sure that during his tenure the Treaty of Paris was signed formally ending the American Revolutionary War." Lord Derby was telling William who was a most attentive listener.

"Do go on Sir. Was the Duke of Portland a friend of yours?"

"Oh, yes he was. Did you know that Portland became one of several vice presidents of London's Foundling Hospital - following in his father's footsteps - one of the most fashionable charities of the era, with several of the nobility serving on its board? He got me involved too. It was founded by Captain Thomas Coram; the hospital's mission was to care for the abandoned illegitimate children of London and about 460 were maintained and educated. Through its deeply moving task it achieved rapid fame with funds raised from an annual exhibition of donated pictures from supporting artists and popular benefit concerts put on by Handel. Later Portland took over the presidency of the charity from Lord North, but I have digressed. Where was I? Sorry, my mind wanders a bit these days. Oh yes, I was out of office but still kept in touch with old Portland and along with other conservative Whigs, he told me he was extremely ill at ease with the French Revolution and parted with Fox over this issue, then joining William Pitt's (Pitt the Younger) government as Home Secretary. I remember it well because that same year there were food riots throughout England due to grain shortages and Portland took part in the movement that refused to eat bread made of more than a determined fineness of wheat in order to save grain. He arranged for substantial numbers of troops to be quartered on the outskirts of London in order to prevent civil unrest."

The port decanter had come round, yet again. William passed it on as he had already consumed what seemed like copious quantities of excellent wine, and he wanted to remember everything that Lord Derby was telling him. Added to that Lizzie would be sure to give him a wigging if he was the worse for wear. It wasn't possible to see across the other side of the table for the fug from the cigar smokers. William didn't smoke and was relieved that Lord Derby had declined one of the fat coronas.

"Yes, it's all coming back to me and I do remember that when he was Home Secretary with responsibility for Ireland, Portland appointed Rockingham's nephew Earl Fitzwilliam as Lord Lieutenant. Then would you believe it, Fitzwilliam announced as government policy that Catholics would be given full equal rights….. best be careful what I say about it in this house. Portland refused to acknowledge the policy and Fitzwilliam was removed from office." Derby lowered his voice and continued "The Irish people felt betrayed by this which resulted in the Irish Rising. Portland then authorised Lord Cornwallis to use whatever means necessary to pass the Act of Union. It was the King's refusal to support Catholic Emancipation that led to Pitt's resignation. Portland then took up the post of Lord President of the Council so that Pelham could become Home Secretary although, apparently, the loss of income caused serious problems for the Duke. Pitt again became Prime Minister and Portland continued in office. Portland, my poor friend, underwent major abdominal surgery to have kidney stones removed. Can you imagine it? I went to see him; he was in a bad way: I thought he would resign from office, indeed I thought he would die, but no, he continued as Lord President of the Council and then as a Minister without Portfolio. I don't know what drove him on with such commitment."

"I understand that you rejoined the ministry" said William.

"Yes, that's right – it was in 1806 – just for a year when The Lord Grenville was PM. It collapsed, you know, and Pitt's supporters returned to power. Portland again became an acceptable figurehead, albeit for a quarrelsome group of ministers, although insisting that he remained a Whig despite the fact that he was heading a Tory government – what a situation! He called and won a general election but then left his ministers to make their own decisions with no guidance from him - that was very strange."

William had to ask "As he seemed so ineffective, why do you think he was such a favourable person for the job?"

"Do you know, I've asked myself that very same question, Lord Longsdon? I think Portland owed his political influence chiefly to his rank, his mild disposition and his personal integrity. He was a good friend to me especially when I went through a troubling time in my personal life."

William could see that Lord Derby was slowing down and had earlier noticed that the elderly man hadn't really eaten anything, had just pushed his food around the plate. "Are you alright, Sir? Have I prevented you from enjoying your meal talking about the past?"

"No, young man, not at all…. just haven't got much of an appetite these days." Lord Derby quickly returned to the question. "To be perfectly honest, his talents were in no sense brilliant and he was deficient in practical energy as well as intellectual grasp. Mind you, I think his state of health greatly sapped his energy. During this second ministry - of course he was quite elderly by then - he presided over a weak government of which he never spoke in a parliament that had started life under a depressing state of military failure during the French Wars. As you well know Napoleon dominated most of Western Europe and went on to conquer the Iberian Peninsula (Spain and Portugal) and so Portland's Government saw the complete isolation of the United Kingdom from the continent. Of course, it's common knowledge what happened next. The Foreign Secretary, George Canning, accused his colleagues of incompetence in their pursuit of the war. Canning was obviously referring to Castlereagh who was the Secretary of State for War and the Colonies and wanted him removed. Portland, as usual, did nothing but other Cabinet ministers took sides - in favour or against Castlereagh. Thus the Cabinet ceased to function. When Castlereagh discovered the conspiracy he demanded 'satisfaction.' He was paranoid and thought himself surrounded by enemies."

Derby paused for a while to enjoy his port.

"Early one morning those two ministers of the Crown in the Duke of Portland's cabinet met to fight a duel on Putney Heath. The challenger, Castlereagh, Minister of War, was a crack shot. George Canning, the Foreign Secretary, had never held a pistol in his life and he believed he had a good chance of being killed. Castlereagh surely could not have wished to kill Canning but it was a near thing as he shot him through the fleshy part of the thigh only a few inches from the femoral artery; he could have bled to death. Both resigned soon afterwards."

"I heard that some years later the mad Castlereagh committed suicide by cutting his throat" remarked William.

Lord Derby nodded his head and continued "the normally calm and patient Portland was furious about the duel and as a result of his rage, suffered a seizure. The poor ministry, rocked by the scandalous duel between Canning and Castlereagh, coupled with his ill health, prompted Portland's resignation. He died a few weeks later heavily in debt; dreadful state of affairs really, all of it. Then, of course, Spencer Perceval became Prime Minister….. It's all in the distant past now.  Do you know, I think I ought to retire to my bed. It's been a good evening; enjoyed meeting you. Hope I haven't bored you."

William had not been bored, totally the reverse but he never could remember, hard as he tried, what they had eaten that evening! Lizzie on the other hand could remember every little detail, not just what they ate for dinner but where everyone sat around the table and the colour and style of all the ladies dresses and jewels. She had enjoyed a wonderful evening.

# 17 CLIPSTONE STREET

# CHAPTER NINE

## Conflicting Beliefs

William Bentinck, Marquess of Titchfield, was a tall, dignified and handsome man. He was known to be virtuous, enjoyed literature and a quiet family life. At the age of eighteen he had publicly recited some verses which were delivered in such a confident manner that immediately identified him as a skilled orator. After his education he and his brother, Edward, made the 'grand tour' and on their return both became members of parliament. As soon as William Bentinck took his seat at the age of twenty four he actively participated in the proceedings of the House which earned him popularity.

When his father died in 1762 William became the third Duke of Portland and then was immediately burdened with an immense financial obligation to his mother, the dowager Duchess, to enable her to continue living in the huge properties and estates settled on her after his father's death. This necessitated him raising money early in his life, a liability which greatly reduced his fortune, ruined his independence and apparently changed his political behaviour.

He had engaged in a couple of romances with notable young ladies before marrying Lady Dorothy Cavendish, the sixteen years old daughter of The Duke of Devonshire of Chatsworth House in Derbyshire and Devonshire House in Piccadilly, London. Burlington House in Piccadilly periodically became available to them as their town residence. The property had come into the possession of the Cavendish family but as they already had a grand house (Devonshire House) just along

Piccadilly they had no need of it. Portland and his brother-in-law Lord George Cavendish each made use of the house for at least two separate spells. But when in London with his wife they mainly resided at Devonshire House or when on his own in his meagre family house in Whitehall. This was an inadequate property in need of repair and in the 1770's he made plans to build a palace to be named Portland House in Cavendish Street opposite Mansfield Street. Because of his lack of funds these grand plans did not come to fruition and much later on by 1805 he had to surrender the lease on the Whitehall house which was then demolished. Nonetheless, Portland was obviously keen to live in Cavendish Square for in 1767 Viscount Weymouth had informed him that Lord Harcourt's House in the square was to be sold (he would not lease out the property) and advised him to apply for it. Weymouth obviously didn't know of Portland's impecunious circumstances! During his two appointments as Prime Minister, as was the custom, he took up residence in Downing Street. He eventually did reside in Cavendish Square but that came about by most unusual circumstances. Harcourt House was the home of the Earl of Harcourt and he foolishly gambled it away. Absolutely everyone played cards in those days. On this occasion it was Portland and Harcourt who were playing; the stakes were very high, Portland won and thus the property came into the possession of the Bentinck family! However the gamble for Harcourt House was cleverly legalized to a leasehold tenancy by the action of the lawyers who stated that the ownership of the mansion could not be separated from the rest of the estate.

The marriage of William Bentinck and Dorothy Cavendish (Duke and Duchess of Portland) produced three daughters and four sons. Sarah Gardom from the little village of Edensor had obviously met them at Chatsworth and afterwards joined the busy household in 1785 when the eldest child of The Portlands was aged seventeen years and the youngest was three or four. Initially, Sarah's precise role within the family is not known and she may have accompanied them to their other stately homes. By this time Portland had already served his first short assignment as Prime Minister from April to December in 1783. He had been known to say "My fears are not that the attempts to perform this duty will shorten my life, but that I shall neither bodily nor mentally perform it as I should."

There appeared to be conflicting sides to his nature. Whilst his involvement with London's Foundling Hospital was admirable and altruistic his involvement with the slave trade was contrary to his public persona - as could be said of many of his peer group. His links with the slave trade and slavery-related issues were mainly through his involvement in the political scene and he was driven by his personal impecunious situation to improve his finances by whatever means possible. When as Home Secretary it is reported that Portland clearly believed that slave-related wealth should be protected as a form of property. (His son, who became the Fourth Duke of Portland, held very different views and became an abolitionist). Evidence was uncovered that Portland had financial interests in slave-trade production although he was not a Caribbean plantation owner or trader himself. However, he did have cousins who were slave-estate owners in Demerara on the north coast of South America.

The Slave Trade began with Portuguese and some Spanish traders taking African slaves to the American colonies that they had conquered in the 15th century. British sailors became involved in the trade in the 16th century; English pirates began selling slaves to the Spanish Colonies. When the British captured Barbados in the West Indies and then secured Jamaica English slave-traders started supplying African slaves to the English colonies and further developments followed in the early 18th century.

For many, such as Portland's contemporary, Peter Thellusson, the slave trade was a great source of wealth and both men considered it to be a necessary foundation of the British Empire. Thellusson regarded the slave-trade as a commodity to be traded and invested in as a means of accumulating wealth; such wealth enabled merchants like him to buy social status, English land and property (part of his fortune was used to build Brodsworth Hall near Doncaster). Portland believed that slaves were a property right, to be defended against the increasing social and political debates on abolition and 'the rights of man.' Societies such as the London Corresponding Society threatened these so called 'rights' by publicly questioning, challenging and demonstrably objecting to doubtful ownership of property and the authority of the government and landed gentry. The fortunes of the privileged and their country houses were commonly closely knit with slavery and the slave-trade. Whereas Thellusson had accumulated and retained great wealth, Portland died heavily in debt; it is thought the reason was because he had lost a fortune in protecting his property and in maintaining his expensive life style as a prominent politician and member of the nobility. Furthermore, Portland had been involved in a prolonged battle with Sir James Lowther over lands in Carlisle which they both claimed as theirs. The case began in August 1767 and continued intermittently for nine years until a final judgement was reached in Portland's favour but by which time he was virtually bankrupt as a result of legal costs. Added to his financial difficulties, in the same year, 1776, he agreed to pay his mother a lease of £16,000 a year (about £1,880,000 today) so he could continue to live at Bulstrode, his mother's property. She meanwhile continued to live at Welbeck Abbey, the vast family seat in the county of Nottingham. Eventually Portland had to sell Cumbrian lands to save himself from bankruptcy.

Sarah Gardom, in her outings around the City of London, must have been aware of the Black and Asian presence (she couldn't really have avoided it). Not just the people she saw but the historical associations with some well-known establishments would have interested or even appalled her. For a long time few people had thought there was anything wrong with slavery and that it was part of Britain's economy, but to Sarah who had not grown up with it in Derbyshire she surely must have felt that it was a great atrocity and a crime against humanity.

Situated in Threadneedle Street was The South Sea Company, a British joint-stock company founded in 1711 and created as a public-private partnership to consolidate and reduce the cost of national debt. The company was also granted a monopoly to trade with South America when Britain was involved in the War of the Spanish Succession and Spain controlled South America. When the war ended in 1713 under the terms of the Treaty of Utrecht Britain gained from France the right, known as the Asiento, to supply 4,800 slaves per year to the Spanish colonies (the West Indies of America belonging to the King of Spain) for a period of thirty years. For the British slave traders it was called the 'triangular trade.' Goods such as guns and brandy could be taken to Africa in exchange for slaves. Those slaves shackled together in chains, with little air, water and food, were taken on the 'Middle Passage' across the Atlantic to be sold in the West Indies and North America. Finally a cargo of rum and sugar was taken back to be sold in England. Inhumane conditions on the middle passage were terrible and many slaves died. The South Sea Company was chosen as the official contractors to carry out the terms of the Asiento regarding the transportation of slaves and had the backing of the Royal family. The warrant for the Indenture, backed by Queen Anne, was put forward by nineteen prominent members of society. Britain was permitted to open offices in Buenos Aires, Caracas, Cartagena, Havana, Portobello and Vera Cruz to arrange slave trade. One ship of general trade goods of no more than 500 tons could be sent to one of those places each year. One quarter of the profit was to be reserved for the King of Spain. By contract with the Royal African Company which supplied the South Sea Company 1,230 slaves were trans-shipped from Jamaica to America in the first year, £10 (about £1,300 today) was paid for a slave over 16 years and £8 (about £1,040 today) for one under 16 but over 10 years. Two thirds were to be male and 90% adult. On arrival of the first cargoes the local authorities refused to acknowledge the Asiento which had still not been officially confirmed by the Spanish authorities. The slaves were sold eventually at a loss in the West Indies. Despite these setbacks the company continued but the trade was unprofitable.

The expectation of vast wealth from trade with South America had been used to encourage the British public to buy shares in the South Sea Company despite the fact that there had been no realistic prospect that trade would take place. The only trade that did take place was in slaves and the company never realised any significant profit from its monopoly. Company shares did rise greatly in value as it expanded its operations dealing in government debt, peaking in 1720 before collapsing at little above its original flotation price. A considerable number of people were ruined by the share collapse and the national economy was greatly reduced as a result. This became known as the South Sea Bubble which caused Britain to rethink its economic policy.

The first Duke of Portland had a heavy involvement with the South Sea Scheme as he had tried to revive his much depleted fortune but the opposite occurred.

\*\*\*

Whatever Sarah's feelings might have been about the unfairness of life for the majority of the population, she could not possibly have expressed an opinion, let alone be seen - even if she had the slightest inclination to do so - with the likes of the London Corresponding Society members as she lived in the household of a prominent member of the nobility and of the government.

# CHAPTER TEN

## A New Life for Sarah

After the resignation, followed very quickly by the death, of His Grace the Third Duke of Portland in October 1809, Spencer Perceval, a small, slight and very pale man, became Prime Minister.

Sarah, at the age of forty seven years, was settling in to her new and comfortable life in Clipstone Street. Her well-proportioned rooms took up the middle floor of number seventeen. On the ground floor was elderly Elizabeth Palmer and next door was James Kerr who was a chair maker with his workshop at the back. Most of the houses had shops or workshops on the ground floor with some stone masons and their yards and a smattering of artist studios. She had found a good butcher, Thomas Jackson, at number eleven and another butcher further along the street who still had all his fingers intact. Mr Flatt was the cheesemonger next door to Mr Fielder at number one who had the whole house and the baker, Mr Greig was on the same side. Anthony Cardon had a very impressive business at number thirty one; he published prints from etched drawings. On the other side of the street was the draper at number two, Mr Hugh Evans, with his lilting Welsh accent and who would engage you in conversation all day if you had the time but he was kind and often gave Sarah small remnants of cloth after she told him she was making a patchwork quilt. Further along was Solomon Isaacs, a glass dealer, whose tiny dark eyes peered over pince-nez precariously balanced on his hook nose, various other houses and trades places including a jeweller, Alexander Rogers (Sarah often gazed at the pretty trinkets in his bay window), three public houses - the noisiest one seemed to be the Half Moon but Sarah was pleased it was at the other end of her street. The most useful craftsman she had found was John Robinson who was a carpenter and joiner and he had helped her hang curtains on new poles and had made and put up some shelves for her.

Financially Sarah was well provided for; she had earned it, kept her side of the bargain. She would remain silent to her dying day. She could not marry, otherwise she would lose her generous annuity, but she thought she might have romance in her life providing she met the right person. Having made one big mistake she had no intention of making another and she had no desire to make a spectacle of herself like Mary Anne Clarke. Everybody knew about that scandal and Sarah had seen the beautiful woman on various occasions. She had been the mistress of Frederick, Duke of York (of 'the Grand Old Duke of York, he had ten thousand men' fame.) and was the daughter of a man named Thompson of Ball and Pin Alley in Chancery Lane. After the death of her father her mother married a compositor named Farquhar who somehow, through connections of his employer, and probably expecting certain favours, managed to give Mary Anne a good education. At the age of twenty two, having already given birth to two children by him, she married a stone mason named Clarke who was from an affluent family. There was no doubt that she was very beautiful and is said to have had a string of affairs and even played Portia at the Haymarket Theatre. Mrs Clarke took a grand house in Gloucester Place, began entertaining lavishly and her name was soon coupled with the Duke of York whereupon she indulged in the wildest extravagances, living very opulently. The Duke, who became her lover, promised her a handsome monthly sum but it was infrequently paid and she was soon pursued by creditors. In order to get money she foolishly promised to use her influence with the Duke, who at that time was commander-in-chief with enormous patronage at his disposal. Because of his easy going nature it was believed by those who knew Mrs Clarke that he would do whatever she wished and for the promise of her influence she received various sums of money, especially from army officers. When it came to public knowledge the man who brought the matter up in the House of Commons in 1809, was named Colonel Wardle. He brought eight charges against the Duke for wrongful use of his military authority. Wardle's period of popularity which followed was short lived; the charges against the Duke were found not proven though there was no doubt that Mrs Clarke had received money for her influence with him. Mrs Clarke gained many admirers for her beauty and courage, even sauciness during the long questioning at the bar of The House. At the end of the investigation the Duke resigned his position of commander-in-chief (to which he returned two years later) and broke off his relationship with Mrs Clarke. The scandal encouraged the production of a hoard of pamphlets, some amusing, most of them false, but the most outrageous of all was Mrs Clarke's own book in which she freely discussed the attitudes of royalty, politicians, various dignitaries and libelling Colonel Wardle who, eventually, prosecuted her and two pamphleteers. They were found 'not guilty' but there was no stopping Mrs Mary Anne Clarke. She then threatened to publish the letters she had received from the Duke. This had to be stopped; Sir Herbert Taylor paid for her silence by buying the letters from her and destroying them (with the exception of one copy deposited at Drummonds Bank). There was still no stopping the woman and she published a libellous letter to the Right Hon. William Fitzgerald. That landed her in trouble and she was sentenced to nine months imprisonment. On her release she went to live in France.

\*\*\*

Sarah's son, John, was in his early twenties and living financially secure in Bolsover in Derbyshire, but she could not reveal to him, or anyone else, her true identity; she had lived with those circumstances for a long time. Being surrounded by artists and artisans, some in Clipstone Street and in nearby Bolsover Street, was the ideal environment for Sarah who was a good needlewoman but now, with the luxury of leisure time and being able to please no-one but herself, decided she would learn to paint and perhaps even write a little poetry. At times she had longed to escape the tense atmosphere of living in a prominent household dominated by politics coupled with the traumatic state of the physical and mental health of the head of the family and, indeed, for a time, the head of the country. Although Portland had appeared outwardly calm and composed during his time as a politician and as Prime Minister (except in those last few weeks of his life) Sarah knew of a different man. Who was it who had massaged his aching shoulders and soothed his sore feet when he returned from a long parliamentary session? His work load was onerous; there was always so much correspondence to deal with, not just parliamentary papers but so many requests and begging letters from constituents, tenants and estate staff and sometimes there was long drawn out litigation.

Despite the restraints put on her personal life she enjoyed her occupation. She had joined the busy and chaotic household as a maid; it was the most unobtrusive role in which she could be employed. It was well known that Sarah could read and write with skill, she had a logical mind and had quickly learnt how to grasp the complexities of a difficult situation and, most importantly, she was discreet. When Portland's secretary had been struck down with a debilitating illness she had longed to take his place, but of course, it wasn't at all feasible for a woman to do so. To be physically close to him was what she had secretly craved. Often Portland worked late into the night dealing with all the paperwork and on one such occasion she had heard a bump in the room below. Feeling her way in the dark she had crept quietly down the back stairs from her attic room, tiptoed along the corridor doing her best to avoid creaking floorboards, through the doorway into the private apartments, seen the light under his study door, tapped on it gently and quietly entered the room. He was down on his hands and knees trying to gather up some papers that had fallen out of the red brief case which had obviously toppled off his huge desk. Calmly she got down and helped him restore everything in an orderly fashion on the desk. Not a word was spoken until she attempted to leave.

"Don't go" was all he had said.

She knew he was tired and ill and when circumstances allowed she surreptitiously comforted him in the quiet hours of the night, distracted him from the troubling matters of state, of riot, of wars and things too numerous to relate. He was usually undemanding, her mere presence and then the touch of her soft mildly fragrant body relaxed him in some strange intoxicating way. She had always respected him, perhaps deeply loved him. Her feelings for him that she could not openly reveal when he nearly died during surgery for the removal of kidney stones almost drove her insane. After his death she had sobbed in isolation; her tears had washed away all her innermost pent up emotions of the previous years. Because of her proud father's actions she had been separated from her family and friends and been swiftly propelled into a new and strange life. But she had accepted the situation - apprehensively at first - she had played her part and now she would stay completely away from politics and anything at all remotely connected with the state of her country!

\*\*\*

After taking his seat in the Commons in 1796 Spencer Perceval's political views were already formed 'he was for the Constitution and Pitt; he was against Fox and France.' Perceval, a lawyer, continued with his legal practise as members of parliament did not receive any salary and The House only sat for part of the year. During the parliamentary recess of the summer of 1797 he was senior counsel for The Crown in the prosecution for sedition of John Binns of the London Corresponding Society. However, Binns, who was defended by Samuel Romilly, was found not guilty. During his time in opposition, Perceval's legal skills were also put to use to defend Princess Caroline, the estranged wife of the Prince of Wales, during a delicate investigation. The Princess had been accused of giving birth to an illegitimate child and the Prince of Wales ordered an enquiry hoping to obtain evidence for a divorce. The government enquiry found that the accusation was untrue and that the child in question had been adopted by the Princess. Perceval made several speeches in The House and gained a reputation as a debater.

In 1812 something happened that could not possibly have escaped Sarah's notice, no matter how hard she tried to ignore politics. As she walked in leafy Marylebone village on her way to buy art materials and noticing the beautiful fresh green leaves of the plane trees and their flowers like pompoms with bursting pollen which made her sneeze, there seemed to be an excited buzz in the air. "Have you heard, have you heard" people were saying "the Prime Minister has been shot!" It was the 11th May - the Prime Minister, Spencer Perceval, had been on his way to the House of Commons to attend a debate and he was assassinated by John Bellingham. Sarah quickly returned home, her purchases could wait for another day. There was a lot of unrest at the time and immediately after the assassination troops were stationed in and around Islington which indicated that a reaction was anticipated. When the news reached the city of Nottingham it was met with scenes of wild jubilation. Times were very unstable, global war broke out a month later when America declared war on Britain and a few days later Napoleon invaded Russia.

But, in actual fact, the assassination had nothing to do with the general angry discontentment of the people. So what on earth had prompted the shooting? Bellingham, a merchant, had a grievance against the government over compensation for unjust imprisonment in Russia. All his petitions had been rejected. It's possible that he was insane. He had bought two pistols for four guineas from Beckwith, a gunsmith just off Smithfield, had made no attempt to escape after the shooting and at his trial only a matter of days later gave no such plea as insanity. He may have been trying to avoid the same experience as his father who was confined for a year in St Luke's asylum in Islington. Less than a month elapsed between Bellingham buying the pistols on 20th April and being imprisoned, tried, executed and his body given to Sir William Blizzard for anatomy at St Bartholomew's Hospital.

Coroners' Inquests were held within forty-eight hours of a suspicious death and were normally conducted at a local alehouse, parish workhouse or in the building in which the death occurred. Deaths among prisoners in custody were also subject to an automatic inquest. In the case of Prime Minister Perceval his body was laid on a sofa in the Speakers drawing room and then removed to Number Ten in the early hours of 12th May. That same morning an inquest was held at the 'Cat and Bagpipes' public house on the corner of Downing Street and a verdict of wilful murder returned.

Most coroners were appointed for life and came from either a legal or medical background. On being notified of a suspicious death the coroner issued a warrant to the local constable instructing him to impanel a jury, usually made up of substantial householders, quite often from the parish in which the death occurred. There were usually up to twenty four members on the jury and juries for prison inquests were made up of half prisoners and half local residents. Witnesses were called to give an account of any circumstances relevant to the death and the depositions of their evidence were written down very rapidly and accurately.

***

Early one morning Sarah could hear a commotion outside in the street as she drew back the heavy gold and rose coloured brocade curtains (they had been given to her by the housekeeper at Harcourt House as they were no longer in use and too good to dispose of) and wondered what on earth was going on. She lifted the sash window and leaned out over the narrow wrought iron balcony to see. It just turned out to be another street crier, this time selling rabbits - no doubt poached, being a crime which carried a drastic punishment - they were tied to a long pole balanced on his shoulder. Perhaps she would buy one another time. That same week she had already seen an itinerant Jewish dealer who bought clothes, usually from servants who were allowed cast offs as perquisites, and then took them to the daily rag fair in Rosemary Lane, which commenced at noon. Sarah had thought that there weren't many servants in Clipstone Street who could give away clothes, but she was wrong. Mary Matthews, servant to Mrs Palmer below, had suddenly appeared in the street with a few items, and there too was Mary Howell servant to Mr Fielder at number one and Mary Murphy had come running along the street from the Half Moon Public House (why were they all called Mary)? There were street vendors all over London, not just in the market place, but hawkers going from door to door selling their wares from a variety of foodstuffs like fresh fish, shell fish, fruit and vegetables, hot pies, plates, pots and pans and even those selling pills and potions claiming to cure all sorts of ailments but whether they ever did was another matter altogether. Many of the street criers offered services such as repairing and caning broken chairs, sharpening knives, cleaning boots and shoes. And of course, there were strolling clowns and entertainers, jesters and many beggars. It was all very noisy, colourful, dirty and smelly!

✳✳✳

He cast an appraising eye over the woman as she entered the room; she looked nervous, but then most of them did. Mmmmm a bit older than he had expected but not skinny – he didn't like them skinny – nicely rounded but not fat. He thought she would do.

"There's a little room over there where you can undress and then come and arrange yourself on the chaise longue."

Sarah was more than flummoxed for a few moments but then quickly regained her composure when she realised that the artist thought she was a model not a pupil. She had joined the local art group and being newly enrolled had turned up early. The studio was approached up a narrow and rickety winding staircase above the gallery. Every inch of wall space was covered in pictures; there were half a dozen sturdy easels placed around the room and various groups of strange objects on tables and ledges - obviously used for still life displays. On one small table was a plate of bread and cheese covered by a glass dome and she wondered if that was lunch or something to paint or both. The floor was covered in an array of mismatched old carpets covered in splodges of paint obviously acquired over a number of years. The wilting geraniums in a large terracotta pot on a windowsill needed water. Had she known this class was life-drawing she might not have turned up, but now it was too late! Mr Oliver apologised profusely and showed her to an easel and said she could use charcoal for her first time as it was more forgiving. (She was glad she had a smock to cover her clothes). In time he said he expected her to be accurate with her drawings; she would soon develop the skill and then she could progress to using paint if she wished; he hoped she would. To begin with she found it quite nerve-racking but soon overcame her lack of experience when she met the other friendly pupils in the class who were naturally very curious about the new lady in the group. And so her different life had begun. As she became more proficient with her drawing she tried portraiture for she saw many interesting characters during her day to day life. Uppermost in her mind was the begging street sweeper, blind in one eye, who was black skinned with white curly hair tied back in a funny little pony tail that stuck out from the back of his head. His fat lips were big and smiling but Sarah didn't know what he had to smile about as his clothes were in tatters and his shoes barely protected his huge, bulbous toed, calloused feet. She wondered where he lived, probably in an alleyway constantly being moved on from doorway to doorway. She had been told about the Jewish religious beggar - a mendicant - offering no service at all, who, apparently being unable to walk, sat in a box on wheels in Petticoat Lane. But she guessed that he had a home and belonged to a family, or more likely lived in the poor house.

A group of Sarah's new friends invited her to join them in a trip to the theatre. The Drury Lane Theatre had burnt down in 1809 but had reopened three years later with a production of Hamlet. The versatile and dishy Robert Elliston was to take the lead part. For a while Sarah was quite interested to follow his progress and saw him in other theatre appearances but was then sad to learn that he became an alcoholic probably brought on by various misfortunes. She knew that people who appeared in the limelight often took to drink but she didn't think she had any fear of that!

# CHAPTER ELEVEN

## The Farmer Duke

William was convinced that His Grace the Third Duke of Portland was the father of Sarah's illegitimate son, John Gardom. From what Mr Binns had told him about Sarah and then marrying up the facts with The Duke's connection with Chatsworth, the time of his residence in London and the fact that Sarah worked in his household until just after the date of his demise it all seemed perfectly logical. William and his sister were discussing the matter. Did anyone in the family know where Sarah had lived and what her life had been like? Had their mother Elizabeth Longsdon known all along and not said anything? Surely there must have been correspondence. Where would they look? Who would know? All they could do was guess. However, there was still a missing piece of the puzzle, as yet unsolved, and ideally they needed to speak to John Gardom, if and when he was willing to do so.

"I'm not so sure that you are right, William, in thinking that the third Duke was John's father" said Lizzie. "You've been away so much looking after your business affairs and you may not be aware that the fourth Duke of Portland is very involved with the Bolsover Estate. Furthermore, people refer to him as 'the farmer Duke.' Father had so rightly concluded all those years ago that John Gardom was a farmer when he saw him in the market selling cattle."

William was trying to do some quick mental arithmetic but he needed to know when the farmer Duke was born. How old was he when Sarah and her baby son left Edensor? Was he the father – surely not? Nonetheless, a good living had been provided for John whoever was the father.

It did not take William much time to establish that the Marquess of Tichfield (like his father his title before ascending the dukedom), the farmer Duke, who was born in 1768, was educated at Ealing and Westminster Schools. It was a well-known fact that the Westminster boys were uncontrolled outside school hours and notoriously unruly about town but the proximity of the school to the Palace of Westminster meant that politicians were well aware of the boys exploits. Then Tichfield attended Christ Church, Oxford where he matriculated in January 1785. However, he was only there for a short time. By all accounts in his boyhood and youth he had been generously indulged by his father.

"I say Lizzie, listen to this," William could not wait to tell his sister "My informant tells me that Tichfield was suddenly taken out of Oxford and sent to The Hague in the Netherlands to gain experience by working with the British envoy Sir James Harris and in the hope that contact with Lady Harris would polish his manners! What do you make of it?"

After some hesitation she answered him by saying that if, at the most impressionable age of seventeen years, he was the father of Sarah's child, he was probably infatuated with her, maybe wanted to marry her. He was too young and she was not a member of the aristocracy; there was probably already someone with wealth lined up for him. Perhaps it had been decided to get him out of the way of her and of any scandal. In which case, somehow Sarah and her family needed to be silenced.

"Yes, and Tichfield didn't return to England until four years later by which time he would have had time to recover from the unfortunate results of his wild behaviour. Huh - most likely he had a good time when he stayed in Paris before returning home" said the thoughtful William.

\*\*\*

Tichfield, or to give him his full title, William Henry Cavendish-Scott-Bentinck, had greatly benefited and matured by his experience of living abroad. He went on to become a politician who served in various positions in the governments of George Canning and Lord Gooderich. He was Member of Parliament for Petersfield and then Buckinghamshire and served under his father as a Lord of the Treasury for a few months in 1807. His political beliefs became more and more liberal; he remained out of office until April 1827 when he was appointed Lord Privy Seal and then Lord President of the Council, an office he retained until the government fell at the beginning of 1828. However, he had no real desire for political office and took little participation in national political life although from his position outside the government he continued to follow politics closely. He was a supporter of the Reform Bill and went on to be a prominent supporter of The Agricultural Protection Group which was formed to campaign in favour of the retention of the Corn Laws. These were trade laws designed to protect cereal producers against competition from less expensive foreign imports. To ensure that British landowners reaped all the financial profits from farming the Corn Laws imposed steep import duties thus making it too expensive for anyone to import grain from other countries even when the people of Great Britain and Ireland needed the food.

After his father died in 1809 Tichfield - but now the fourth Duke of Portland - found that the estates he had inherited were burdened with debt. He became heavily involved with the management of those estates and was highly successful in reversing the financial situation. He gained a reputation as an agricultural improver as he was particularly interested in farming methods and techniques and undertook several drainage schemes at Welbeck. Added to his farming interests he was involved with the development of Troon Harbour in Ayrshire, Scotland, and the railway construction which linked to it. His interests did not end there. Through his study of shipbuilding and design he arranged a few trials with the Admiralty in which his own and other private yachts competed with some of the fastest ships in the navy. He also loved horse racing, was a tenant of the Jockey Club at Newmarket and was responsible for many improvements to the turf, the gallops and the building of the Portland stand.

The fourth Duke of Portland, or Farmer Duke, had indeed married a rich heiress, Henrietta, daughter of General John Scott and his wife Margaret (nee Dundas), in London in 1795 and they went to live at Welbeck, (the third Duke, before his death, preferring to remain in London close to his political commitments and at Bulstrode during periods of parliamentary recess). At the time of his marriage he obtained Royal Licence to take the name "Scott" in addition to that of Bentinck. By all accounts it was a very happy marriage and they were parents of nine children. It became increasingly difficult to tempt him away from Welbeck after his marriage and when he ascended the Dukedom he sold Bulstrode Park in Buckinghamshire.

***

William was keen to see John Gardom again, he badly wanted to know where the man had spent his childhood and youth and, on impulse, decided to return to Bolsover, telling his sister he would have to find overnight accommodation as it was too far to travel there and back in one day; it wouldn't hurt to see what trade was like in the market and by chance he might just bump into John!

"I'm beginning to think that you have found yourself a lady friend" had teased his sister.

"No such luck" he had replied.

Nor did William have any luck in seeing John, it was a silly wild-goose chase and he definitely wasn't going to make an impromptu visit to his house. He stopped again at The Blue Bell Inn situated in the High Street, or Upper Street as it was frequently called, which he had easily found before at the top of Market Street, where they stabled, fed and watered his trusty steed, a beautiful Cleveland Bay, and he knew he would get nourishing food for himself. Richard Revill, the landlord, assured William he would be well looked after and that the usual local crowd in that night were a friendly bunch. After buying a few drinks for local farmers he had seen in the market he enquired if any of them knew John Gardom and was told he was often seen trading his livestock, but he was a real loner who never had much to say and never came into the tap room for a drink even though he lived nearby. Jessie appeared briefly from the kitchen and welcomed him back. William quickly got into conversation with a couple of locals and heard a strange tale about the new residents of Bolsover Castle.

The Duke of Portland was renting out Bolsover Castle to the Reverend John Hamilton-Gray, curate of Bolsover and his wife, Mrs Hamilton-Gray had been known to write to a friend that 'honour and principle does not seem to be known in the place and we soon found that drunkenness and unchastity were not considered crimes, except in the clergy. The former was reckoned good fellowship and the latter a common and very excusable misfortune!' She found it a philistine and isolated village. They were a civilised couple who frequently spent their winters on the continent mixing with minor European Royalty and Mrs H G developed a sort of love hate relationship with the town, castle and local population, the latter which she found rough and boorish.

Reverend W.C. Tinsley was the vicar at the time, a man miserably addicted to intemperate habits and who sometimes entered the pulpit on Sunday with a black eye, resulting from a scuffle in which he was engaged during Saturday evening. The Bishop obviously regarded it desirable that Tinsley be dispossessed of the living of Bolsover but took the easy way out and bargained with the man that so long as he would accept a Curate of the Bishop's choosing (Hamilton-Gray) then he could remain as Vicar, enjoying the income of £100 per annum, leaving the Curate with the surplice fee only. Hamilton-Gray's position was fairly unusual in that he was a 'gentleman' - in other words he had independent means and was not wholly reliant on his stipend.

The Hamilton-Grays set up home in the castle, which, according to Mrs H G, was 'the only house they could find fit for a gentleman's residence in the parish.' Vicar Tinsley, with a payment of £25 removed himself to the Vicarage from the Castle were he had lived with his wife in two of the rooms whilst the children inhabited the kitchen and offices. When Dyson, the Chesterfield upholsterer, arrived to discuss furnishings with the new Curate and Mrs Hamilton-Gray he found Tinsley being chased along the terrace by his wife who was wielding a carving knife, whilst he retreated with a bucket full of water ready to throw at her when she came near! On the second occasion of Dyson's visits the doors were barred against him as Tinsley had mistaken him for the Bailiff who was expected at any minute to take away the furniture.

"Let's have another round of drinks" said William, interrupting the story teller and was then told that, as to be expected, the castle was in a pretty disgusting state; the servants refused to let Mrs H G below stairs for a week until they disposed of the filth. No-one had really occupied the building properly since the Countess of Oxford had stripped the Terrace Roof of its timbers and furniture in the early 1750's. The part of the castle known as The Little Castle was occupied by the Hamilton-Grays and although not a ruin it had never been lived in by the Dukes of Portland. Skirting boards were missing, windows loose down off their hinges or removed altogether, with boards nailed together to keep out the draughts. Pictures left by the Duke and not wanted at Welbeck Abbey were shot through with arrows and around the outside of the castle under the drawing room windows was a smelly, festering swamp. According to Mrs H G there was not a shrub or tree about the windy place and no path, far less a road. The whole place made her shudder but her husband could see beyond the ruins and squalor to the stately pile the building originally was. He was known to have said that there was nothing too vulgar about the place that could not be remedied. "You will not find monumental chimney pieces, frescoed walls, arched cupolas and a marble boudoir in other parsonages, and if we should care to remain here you will like it as much as I do" he told his wife. She remained unconvinced. The one attraction for her was the fact that within a short distance from the castle were four titled families whom she thought she could socialize with!

Between mouthfuls of food William Longsdon was further regaled with the saga. Conditions within the town when the Hamilton-Grays arrived were at an all-time low - physically, morally and spiritually. The church was attended by a handful of people although considering the ministrations of Reverend

Tinsley it is surprising they found any congregation at all. The school contained six boys, all of whom were paid for by Lady Oxford's Charity.

This was a long and thirsty tale and William was pleased to have a bed for the night.

"The two church wardens are over there" said one of the ruddy faced whiskered men at his table "Bradley and Clarke. Bradley's daughter keeps house for her father – the latest gossip is that her illegitimate daughter is by the village doctor and her husband has moved in with someone else, but a very respectable woman. Clarke is a farmer with an income three times as much as the Vicar but he has been very helpful to the Hamilton-Grays, helping them to settle in. It's scandalous, though, what he's done. Eeh my word, that was good beef pudding wasn't it (he emitted a hearty belch) and, oh yes, when he got married Clarke persuaded his father in law, who lives next door to him, to part with all his savings, making him a pauper, and therefore he's eligible for parish relief….. would you believe it, but most people round here think it was a clever and natural thing to do!"

By that time William had drank and heard enough, thanked his 'new friends' for their entertaining company and found his way up the creaky old stairs to his temporary bed. He thought that for Hamilton-Gray to stay in such an alien and even hostile environment said much for his strength of character and religious beliefs.

✱✱✱

He was soaking wet; even the greatcoat had not kept out the driving rain as he had ridden back through a tremendous storm. His legs were sore where his breeches had clung to and rubbed his inner thighs. Before doing anything else he needed to give his tired horse a good rub down and some decent food.

Because he was so impetuous William had wasted a journey to Bolsover. He felt guilty. Before leaving, however, he managed to purchase some very fine lace for his sister for her to trim a dress. He determined to be less impulsive about the mystery of Sarah Gardom and her son John.

# 17 CLIPSTONE STREET

# CHAPTER TWELVE

## Mourning

John Binns was finding it difficult to cope with the loss of Sarah. He wandered round his house like a lost soul, he could not eat and he lay awake at night thinking about her, about all their good times together. He missed everything about her especially their physical closeness. He thought of the time when they had gone to a see a strange play. They had been to the theatre a few times, but Sarah asked to see Edmund Kean who was giving his first performance as Sir Giles Overreach in Massinger's play 'A New Way to Pay Old Debts.' The drama was riveting, Kean's performance reached heights never scaled before and he was so frightening that Mrs Glover playing the part opposite him was terrified to such an extent that she fainted on stage! John had protectively put his arm around Sarah who had been quite affected by it all. Even he at one stage had gripped the edge of his seat. At the end of his role the stunned audience shortly regained its composure and the tension was relieved by yelling and roaring for Kean, giving him an ovation never seen in Drury Lane before.

It was the first time he had taken Sarah back to his house in Windsor Terrace. He had planned it. His little sitting room on the first floor was cosy, the fire embers still glowing. He had already set up a small table and two chairs and his housekeeper had prepared a warming supper as requested. The candles in their silver sticks were ready to be lit and he had chosen the wine carefully. His memory of the short carriage journey from the theatre was vague but he knew that since the realistically terrifying performance Sarah had remained very close to him.

He removed her muff and fur trimmed cloak and she allowed him to kiss her - her upturned face was begging for him to do so. He kissed her slowly and her lips parted under his. He forgot about the wine; he slowly traced his fingers down her spine and momentarily rested his hand in the small of her back. He felt her yield to his body. Her arms were around his neck and they were soon kissing passionately. When they undressed he cannot remember. She was everything he desired; he lost himself in her sensual kisses and caresses, they didn't even reach the adjoining bedroom - made exquisite love in front of the fire climaxing in heights he had never known before. Afterwards she had worn his silk dressing gown whilst they ate their supper and drank the wine. It was their first glorious, ecstatic time; he would always remember.

On occasions John and Sarah walked in the Royal Vauxhall Gardens admiring the tree lined avenues, the rococo buildings and water fountains. Beautifully dressed promenaders were sometimes entertained by the music of Handel or other composers popular at the time. He loved it in summer when she wore the powder blue empire line dress (his favourite), a satin ribbon tied in a bow above her waist and with diaphanous sleeves through which one could glimpse little puff sleeves at the top of her dainty arms. She had a matching parasol; all the ladies had them and she would sometimes wear a lace trimmed bonnet. He had given her a fine woollen stole of many colours to drape round her shoulders on chilly days or evenings. She had started wearing shoes with Louis heels; they were becoming fashionable for men too but he didn't wear them as he thought they were for dandies. Thank goodness wigs for men were no longer in vogue and he liked the straight pants to the ankle rather than breeches and stockings; it was all much simpler to deal with. His tailor had made him a new coat with a fashionable stand up collar, fairly wide shoulders and slightly nipped in at the waist which made him feel that he was an acceptable masculine shape. In the evenings hundreds of lanterns that hung from the Vauxhall Gardens trees were lit. One of the star attractions once was when the French tightrope walker, Madam Saqui, with a head dress of enormous plumes of ostrich feathers, danced sixty feet above them whilst fireworks crackled around her. John imagined that even if she had slipped she would have just floated gently down to earth.

Sometimes Sarah cooked delicious little suppers at Clipstone Street after their outings but she never encouraged him to stay the night. Although their relationship was not a clandestine affair John understood that she wished to retain her good reputation and respectable demeanour. But Sarah often went to stay with him at Windsor Terrace; his residence was more private and not overlooked by prying neighbours.

They went again and again to the Royal Academy to see the painting by Sir David Wilkie: 'The Chelsea Pensioners Reading the Waterloo Despatch' which depicted the victory of Waterloo, the battle that had brought to an end the Napoleonic Wars. There was absolutely no doubt that it was a remarkable painting in colour and detail and the facial expressions of the entire street conveyed the response to the good news.

On one occasion Sarah had asked to see where he worked in Threadneedle Street and they had done a little tour round that side of London.

It had been unintentional but they found themselves in Lombard Street looking at the wall monument to John Newton on the side of Woolnoth Church. Newton had been sent away to school which he found an unhappy experience and by the age of eleven he was serving on his father's ship sailing to the

Mediterranean. When his father retired, plans were made for young Newton to work on a sugar plantation but instead he signed on with a merchant ship. The following year, whilst on his way to visit friends he was captured and press ganged onto the Royal Naval ship HMS Harwich. At one point he attempted to desert and was punished in front of the whole crew of 350. Stripped to the waist and tied to the grating he received a flogging of eight dozen lashes and then was reduced from the rank of midshipman to common seaman. He considered murdering the captain and then committing suicide by throwing himself overboard but fortunately he recovered his mental and physical strength. Later he transferred from 'Harwich' to 'Pegasus,' a slave ship bound from India with goods to West Africa to be exchanged for slaves to be shipped to England. Newton caused trouble for the crew and they left him in West Africa with a slave dealer who gave him to his wife, an African duchess, where he was abused and mistreated along with other slaves. By 1748 he was rescued by a sea captain, who had been asked by Newton's father to search for him, and he returned to England on the ship 'Greyhound.' The following year again on board the same ship on its way from Brazil back to London most of the crew survived a terrible storm in the Atlantic but were blown off course to Northern Ireland. Apparently he felt he had been saved by God from a near-death experience. Whilst waiting in Ireland for the ship to be repaired he was a guest at a shooting party when he accidently discharged his gun narrowly missing his own head. This second near-death experience convinced Newton that God was watching over him and he converted to Evangelical Christianity. Although he professed to have strong Christian beliefs he continued his work with the slave-trade. Some said that he was a fervent campaigner against slave trade having had first-hand experience and he did renounce the business of slave-trade much later in his life. His latter journeys may have been in a pastoral role as the appointed member of the Clergy required aboard in order to accompany each slave ship.

Sarah had been prompted to ask about the slave trade because they were in a small area of the City where there was a wealth of related history.

John took her to see the site of the first Coffee House, The Pasque Rose, built in 1652 in St Michaels Alley. The whole alley was destroyed by the great fire of London but a new establishment named the Jamaica Coffee House was built afterwards; the name Jamaica probably referred to Britain's recent acquisition of the island of Jamaica with its sugar plantations. At one time London had over two thousand coffee houses, being places where traders met to discuss business and arrange loans, advertise the sale of slaves or put up notices for the capture of runaway slaves. A notice for 1728 showed a two guinea reward for a runaway Black female slave.

Sarah had shuddered and told John that she thought her employers had long ago made money from the slave trade. She had seen extracts from an old account dated 1686 of the slave ship 'Pelican' for sales of slave Negroes for the Royal African Company of England. It was permanently ingrained on her memory and revealed individual prices invoiced to customers for its 'cargo.' She could remember that the amount paid for 146 slaves, including freight and provisions amounted to nearly £2,000.00 (about £290,000 today).

They had walked round the corner into Leadenhall Street where during the reign of Elizabeth I the East India Company had been set up to expand Britain's trade in spices and other goods with the Indian subcontinent. The company's influence in India had grown rapidly; a situation which the British government found difficult to control. Investors, together with company employees, were able to accumulate wealth quickly and lived luxurious lifestyles. After working in India many people brought Asian servants back to Britain.

Situated a few doors away was Africa House. Originally this was the headquarters of The Company of Royal Adventurers, which received a royal charter from King Charles II but it became the Royal African Company, again by Royal charter. Its principal aim was to develop the African slave trade and ensure that Britain received its share of profits from the transatlantic slave trade and other goods from Africa.

The afternoon of that outing had been one of the few times that John had glimpsed a serious side of Sarah's nature and as far as he could remember it was the only time that she had referred to her employers, The Portland family.

For much of the time when he was working Sarah happily occupied herself with her fine needlework and perfecting her painting and drawing and sometimes with his encouragement getting her work framed.

Those few happy years they had spent together had slipped by so quickly and John was anxious to recapture and savour as many of his memories that he could.

***

In July, 1830 William received a letter from Mr Binns:

Dear William,

Thank you for your letter. I am sorry to hear that you have been unable to make contact again with John Gardom, but it is early days; only a short time since your visit to me in Windsor Terrace. You will, I am sure, hear from him sooner or later, and yes, I would very much like to come to Little Longstone to meet him and your family when that time eventually arrives.

There was so little time to tell you about Sarah when you were here but there were many years of her life which were a mystery to me. However, there is one thing I must tell you. When she moved to Clipstone Street Sarah pursued her love of painting and we sometimes went together to see exhibitions of great contemporary artists in London. One such time was to an exhibition at the Royal Academy of work by Charles Hayter who was gaining a rapid reputation as a painter of miniature portraits. Sarah admired his ability to get a good likeness with quick pencil sketches. I could see that he was flattered by her interest in his work, by her technical questions and he revealed to her how he placed the sketches behind the transparent ivory in order to paint the little pictures with his clever use of colour. He asked for my permission to paint her portrait; perhaps he thought that she was my wife but as her companion, of course, I readily agreed and as a result Sarah duly went to his studio nearby in St Marylebone to sit for her portrait. What I didn't tell Sarah at the time was that when she was engaged in conversation with other admirers of his work, I commissioned him to paint a miniature portrait of her for me. The exquisite little painting on ivory - now in a gold frame - is with me constantly. Since Sarah died at the end of last year I have missed her so much and I carry it in my breast pocket. You will see the precious item when I come to Little Longstone and, at least, John will be able to see how lovely his mother was. I do not think I can part with it as yet.

Please be assured that I will always be pleased to see you when business affairs bring you to London and that my home is at your disposal where I trust you will find the accommodation more comfortable than the local coaching inn.

I remain your good friend

John Binns.

# CHAPTER THIRTEEN

**Bolsover - Late Summer, 1830**

He had walked back up the steep fields at the back of his house and was slightly out of breath. At long last he had got the cow to accept the new calf along with her own. It had all taken longer than he anticipated but in the long run it would save time; it was the preferable way and saved the nuisance of having to strip milk off the cow and then feed the calf, first of all by getting it to suck his fingers in the bucket of milk. He had bought the little animal in the market that morning; it was healthy but had looked so pathetic in the corner of the cattle pen and he had carried it home wrapped round with a sack. With luck and patience there was money to be made with rearing calves and it was something he often did. There was always so much to do but he liked it that way and he was generally happy with his lot. It never ceased to amaze him how generous his guardian had been in setting him up with a house and a living. But now he was brooding about the recent business regarding his mother and Margaret was getting frustrated with him. He went into his workshop to occupy himself for a while.

"Husband, when are you going to stop walking round this trunk? It's been stuck here for days; someone will fall over it and break an arm or leg. Let's open it; I'm sure the contents won't bite you."

"Don't raise your voice to me like that, Margaret, I'm not deaf" John retorted.

Margaret had gone into the workshop where John was repairing a spindle-back chair. The children had been too rough in their play and broken the comfortable arm chair which, because of its small size, was a favourite for Margaret to sit in. Her feet did not dangle as was usually the case with most chairs.

John Gardom of Bolsover was going quite deaf and sometimes he used his deafness to his own advantage. Margaret was such a patient woman.

"Come on, now the children are in bed, let's do it. I'm dying to see what Mr Binns has sent from London" said his wife.

"Give me a few minutes - I've nearly finished - just need to clamp this together" said John. He was a practical man; making and repairing things gave him pleasure and satisfaction.

"I'll bring the trunk on the sack-truck into the kitchen and you can open it."

The sturdy chest had been sent via a carrier obviously at great cost. It contained a short letter from John Binns explaining that these were Sarah's belongings that he had removed to his house for safe-keeping after her death. Margaret was very excited by it; neither of them had realized that there were more possessions to come from John's mother. They had been both delighted and puzzled by the little silver watch with its tender message engraved inside the back of the case. And now there were further items which had belonged to the mysterious lady.

"Oh look, more paintings….. and a patchwork quilt - that will be useful. Something wrapped up here: what a lovely stole - it has a delicate faint perfume - and there's a little note attached; I'll read it later" said Margaret who felt as if in smelling the perfume she had momentarily come very close to her mother-in-law and that she was almost in the room with them.

John overcame his reluctance, forgot his misery and became interested at last. "There's a lot of packaging material, must be something fragile……be careful, where shall we put this pretty blue and white cup and saucer? It's got red lettering on the base and there are more pieces. It's a wonder it didn't get broken, but there are picture frames strategically placed. Mr Binns packed it very carefully. How very decent of him to send Mother's effects; we'd have been none the wiser if he'd kept them. Here, something I have always wanted - a little carriage clock in a leather case and, Margaret, for you an ostrich feather fan."

Margaret didn't say what was in her mind, that they never went to such places where she could use a fan. They didn't go anywhere. Even if there was a play house nearby John probably wouldn't be able to hear half of what was said. She could see her husband was quite overwhelmed; he had used the word 'Mother.' These were the precious belongings of his mother whom he had not known. He then unwrapped a pair of cranberry coloured port glasses. Margaret washed them and produced from her cupboard a bottle of damson wine; she thought they should celebrate and John needed to talk and release his pent up emotions. There were still more lovely things in the chest to discover. They bent over to carefully empty it. There were some lace handkerchiefs and a small quantity of dainty table linen. They admired the hand embroidered pillow cases. There were some glass rummers (one was cracked) and then something that really did surprise them - almost at the bottom was a pair of silver candlesticks engraved with a family crest.

They placed all the pieces of blue dragon painted china on the table; there was enough for two people – perhaps enough for a couple having romantic suppers. Margaret could see that the maker was Grainger Lee & Co., Worcester. John was trying to decipher a note but handed it to his wife "I can't make it out; will you read it to me?"

It was in the most beautiful writing that Margaret had ever seen: "It says: Chasing the flaming pearl. In Asia the dragon is revered as a divine mythical creature, a potent symbol of strength, good fortune and transformation and is often portrayed chasing a luminous pearl. The dragon seems to be reaching out to clutch the elusive object; swirling through mists and shadows, mouth open and eyes bulging in anticipation of achieving the prize often identified as ball lightening, the sun, the moon or rolling thunder."

John looked intently at the exquisitely illustrated note painted with the blue dragon just like the china. He was impressed and said "she must have really loved this pattern; it would have cost a lot of money. There is a brightly coloured silk cushion too with a dragon in the centre. We must treasure these things. Will you display the china on the dresser with your Willow Pattern plates? It's like Christmas when I was a little boy before I went to live on the farm. Where was she then? Who was my father? I need to know. I would like to see Mr Binns and I would like to go to Little Longstone to visit William and find out about my relatives. Have I got brothers and sisters? It feels so strange. I did not think I belonged to anyone at all. Do you think your parents would come and look after the children for us?"

# CHAPTER THIRTEEN

Little Longston Manor

# CHAPTER FOURTEEN

**Little Longstone Manor - Autumn 1830**

Bates appeared at the scullery door looking perplexed.

"Is The Master here," he asked the kitchen maid "only there's a piece of machinery been delivered and I haven't the faintest idea what it is or what I'm to do with it."

William had heard his farm manager and came to his rescue.

"Now don't you worry, Bates, just carry it round to the lawn at the front of the house and I will demonstrate its use. We'll no longer have to get one of the men to use a scythe to cut the grass….. watch me."

From behind the machine William pushed it up and down the lawn. It was about 19 inches wide with a frame made of wrought iron and the cutting blades on one of the rotary cylinders neatly cut the grass and the clippings were hurled forward into a tray like box at the front.

"Well I never," said the astounded Bates. "What a marvellous thing. Where did you find it?"

William explained that his London agent had heard about the invention of the lawn mower by a man named Budding and the rotating action was based on the rotating blades he had observed in the cloth mill where he worked and William, of course, knew where the wrought iron frames could be made. It was as simple as that. All they needed now was to find where the set of ninepins had been stored and that would probably take longer than cutting the grass!

***

It was one of those rare, warm, early autumn days. A table and chairs had been set out on the lawn in the stone walled enclosed garden at the front of Little Longstone Manor. Lizzie had insisted that some of the rooms were redecorated and her housemaids had cleaned the whole house. She had gone to great lengths to make the two guest bedrooms look welcoming with crisp white bed linen and bowls of rose petal potpourri made that summer. She could not remember the last time they had entertained overnight guests and she thought it was going to be quite fun. Making the arrangements had been like setting the scene for a play. Mr Binns had arrived the previous evening and was still sleeping after his long journey. William hadn't told her how charming and handsome he was. The children had been told that if they behaved themselves they could play ninepins after luncheon on the immaculate lawn, meanwhile, they were totally engrossed with a wooden jigsaw puzzle that Mr Binns had brought them. When they had managed to piece it all together he said they would see that it was a picture of Buckingham House in London. John and Margaret Gardom were due to arrive within the hour.

There was probably far too much food but better to have too much than run out. The farm manager's wife, Mrs B, had kindly helped them out. She loved cooking and Lizzie wasn't used to providing large quantities; in fact the thought of it made her feel very nervous. Mrs B had done the ham with molasses just how they liked it and the turkey was still cooking nicely. On the cold slab in the larder were all manner of delicious things including freshly whipped cream to accompany fruit pies. Lizzie knew the pies would just melt in the mouth for Mrs B made the best pastry for miles around; everyone hoped they would get her apple pie at the harvest supper.

"I'll just stay and help, make sure it all runs smoothly. No need to worry your head about a thing, Miss Elizabeth" Mrs B had said in her reassuring way. "You just enjoy your visitors."

***

John and Margaret Gardom obviously seemed a little nervous to begin with; they were not used to mixing with 'company.' But they soon felt at ease after their journey with a welcoming drink of Lizzie's elderflower wine. They had brought some damson wine and Sage Derby cheese with them; the only gifts they could think of. Margaret immediately fell in love with the beautiful old manor house and John was looking forward to seeing round the farm. Mr Binns, wearing country tweeds, had been introduced to them. William thought how different he looked. He also noticed the slightly flushed complexion of his sister - well, well! William and Lizzie had decided that they wouldn't ask too many questions of John and Margaret; they didn't want it to seem like an inquisition and it was quickly apparent that John Gardom had impaired hearing, so it was best to let him do most of the talking.

John informed them that he was sent to a good school by his guardian with the hope of gaining a sound education but he found lessons difficult. He could hear alright then, he was good at arithmetic and he had learnt the alphabet but the words in books always seemed jumbled up. Mr Binns asked him which school it was and the reply was a big surprise to them all:

"We had a tutor at home for a while and then from the age of seven I attended the Great Ealing School in London - all the boys in the family did. It was in an old rectory – a moated house with a magnificent garden which stood next to the Church. There was a swimming pool, cricket greens, tennis courts and fives courts. I remember a row of cottages that were used as studies and opposite was the parish workhouse where the poor and infirm slept three or more to a bed. I didn't dare misbehave; it had been instilled in me from an early age that as an orphan I was very fortunate and could have started life at the Foundling Hospital and ended up working at the age of seven and living in the poor house. Besides, my guardian was a member of parliament and very involved with the charity school. As I grew up it always puzzled me why I wasn't at the Foundling Hospital but I had quickly learnt that the best policy was not to question anything!"

After a couple of years struggling with school John explained that it was decided that he should go and live on a farm. He loved all the sport and outdoor activities at school and it was apparent that he loved animals as they had Newfoundland dogs in the grand London house and, big and strong as they were, he could make them do anything he wanted. He and another boy in the household, Walter, were sent to the Home Farm near Bolsover where the kindly farmer and his wife had no children and that's where both the boys lived happily, learning useful skills and a new and satisfying way of life away from the noise and dirt of the city. There they worked until they each got married. Walter moved away but John moved into the house where he and Margaret still resided. Mr Binns, Lizzie and William were almost holding their breath wondering what was coming next. William had to ask the question:

"Where did you live in London?"

"Some of the time in Piccadilly - we moved about a bit- but my guardian and the family eventually moved to Cavendish Square. I never visited but I'm told it was very grand although ugly and draughty. I've never been back to London, never had any reason to."

To William it was all beginning to make sense. "Was it Harcourt House?"

"Yes, that's right. How did you know?"

"Was the Duke of Portland your guardian?"

John nodded.

Almost as if he had forgotten, or he was waiting for the right moment, Mr Binns withdrew a little leather pouch from his inside breast pocket and carefully extracted the cameo. Trembling and with baited breath he showed it to John.

"Oh, I remember that lady, she was very kind to me…. .it's Sarah Green. How did you get this? She was always with the family. She used to take me to school….. she seemed very upset when I left to go to the farm."

No-one else could speak. Lizzie was overcome and cried. Margaret guessed and cried too.

John looked at them all and then he stuttered:

"Is she my mother? …………….. Why, why, why didn't I know?"

Margaret and Lizzie disappeared into the house to dry their eyes and found Mrs B dabbing her eyes with the corner of her apron. They returned with the damson wine.

Mr Binns wanted to tell them everything that he could remember about Sarah Gardom.

William was very sad but decided that the next day he would take John to Gardom Edge to look across at Edensor, Baslow and Chatsworth and the farm below which is where it had all begun many years ago.

# EPILOGUE

**Chapter 2**

Bubnell Hall, the home of Johnathan Gardom and his daughter Elizabeth before she married James Longsdon, still stands today. Calver Mill continued in operation until the early 1920's when the mill was then closed down. During World War II the empty building was put to use as a storage depot while the yard became the scene of a crushing and washing plant for fluorspar. After the war the premises were adapted for the manufacture of stainless steel sinks. The building was used for the filming of 'Colditz' and the site has now been converted to luxury apartments.

**Chapter 3**

The home of Anna and Richard Oddy, Bubnell Old Hall, still stands today.

Woodhouse, the original farmhouse underneath Gardom Edge, was replaced with The Yeld Farm, built against the new Sheffield Road in about 1803. The Gardom family continued to farm there well into the 1880's.

The name of Christopher's wife, Rachel, is fictitious.

**Chapter 6**

Clipstone Street and much of Marylebone have been rebuilt.

**Chapter 8**

Anaesthetics had not been discovered when The Duke of Portland had abdominal surgery.

The Third Duke of Portland was also the great-great-great grandfather of Queen Elizabeth II through her maternal grandmother.

Lord Derby died in 1834

## Chapter 9

Devonshire House was demolished in 1924

Eventually changes in the inequalities of peoples' lives came about but Sarah did not live long enough to see the reconstruction of the whole system of government. Emancipation of the slaves in the West Indies occurred in 1833, four years after she died. The English government awarded educational grants to religious societies, The Poor Law was reformed and the first Factory Act was passed. Life for the ordinary working man, especially those not so fortunate and able-bodied was beginning to improve.

## Chapter 11

Mrs Hamilton-Gray never did get to socialize with her titled neighbours!

When the Hamilton-Grays first went to Bolsover the Church was attended by only a handful of people. It was to the H Gs' great credit that the congregation eventually grew to three hundred.

John and Margaret Gardoms' son, George, was one of six boys who attended Bolsover School. Forty years later numbers had risen to 180 scholars.

Mrs H G started a reading and writing class for working class women. Reverend H G had taken over as vicar from Tinsley in 1833 (although in practise he had been doing the job for four years) and at the same time the living of Scarcliffe was conferred upon him providing a much improved income from two parishes. The H Gs then set about converting the 'windy, rambling, desolate looking Norman Castle (the building known as the little castle) into a habitation fit for civilised man.' They added a porch and outer door to the east so that they could take exercise in bad weather without the need to venture onto the open terrace. Below the exposed castle walls they planted trees to act as a windbreak. They built doors and staircases, altered fireplaces in smoky rooms, added double windows on the windy side and generally created a house which could be lived in; until then the castle had not been properly inhabited for eighty years. During the two years that it took to complete the work they also installed stoves in Scarcliffe and Bolsover Churches and worked on the Bolsover school house.

John and Margaret Gardom, who raised six children, resided in their farmhouse in Bolsover until their deaths followed by their unmarried daughter (who took a lodger) until she died in 1894.

## Chapter 14

Relatives of the Longsdon family still reside at Little Longstone Manor surrounded by the village houses and cottages. It is a place where time seems to have stood still.

Visit Gardom Edge if you ever have the opportunity.

## Bibliography

Adapted story of the Hamilton-Grays in Chapter Eleven 'This Windy, Rambling, Desolate Looking Castle' from 'More Bolsover Remembered' written by Bernard Haigh.

Thanks to Derbyshire Records Office, Bolsover Library, and Dr David Dalrymple-Smith for their help.

Factual information extracted from Encyclopaedia Britannica (Ninth edition).

## About the Author

Ann Carmichael lives in Worcestershire with her husband. Both 'The Ironmaster' and '17 Clipstone Street' have evolved after researching the life of her ancestors, the Gardom family, who for centuries lived in the Derbyshire Peaks. It took five years of searching through records before anything about Sarah Gardom was found and that was a moment of great joy.